HAI

C.Taylor

BOOKS

Ted Kelly: The Best Bloke Ever
Copyright Courtney Taylor 2023.
Published by C. Taylor Books
Courtney Taylor asserts all moral rights over this work.
First edition 2023.
ISBN: 978-0-9941605-7-7

TED KELLY

THE BEST BLOKE EVER

The Man, The Message, The Musical - without music

by Courtney Taylor

Y'SEE...

Ted Kelly was born a thousand years ago
    (In fact it might have been a smidgen more)
    In a country known as Aus, and it's named that because
    Well, its residents they brandished a saw

And they lopped off the back part of a word that made tongues smart
    You see *Australia* is laborious to repeat
    So they whittled it away (as they do with *Goodeth day*)
    To a nub that still conveys conceptual meat

Now before this story leaps aflight
     There are some things to understand
     About the customary protocols
     Of the citizens of this land
     The Aussies long have firm avowed
     If a debt is owed it's owed
     And if the sum pertains to violence
     Either more or cash be showed

A perpetrator must find oneself
    Dealt the equivalent of one's crime
    And if they manage to dodge the blow
    A relative cops the slime
    In the city we now focus on
    In the backwaters of Aus
    Muck was often thrown about
    Usually simply *just because*
    There was violence, there was chaos
    But there was method, make that note
    In fact the Aussies so esteemed their ways
    They were often wont to gloat.
    Their widespread application
    Of violent retribution
    In fact produced a system
    To moderate stabbin'-shootin'

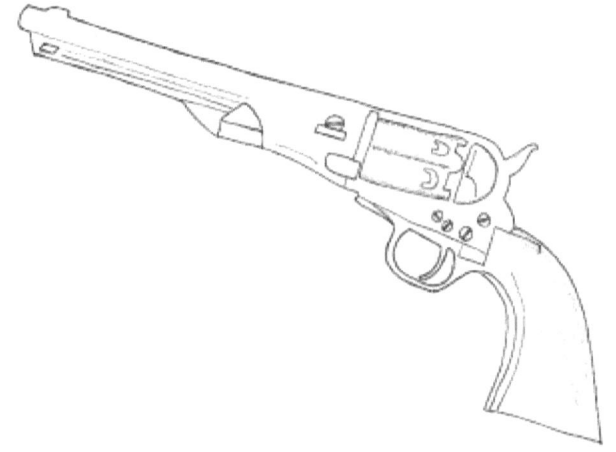

Haemo-cash is what they call
    The payments that are made
    To the still-remaining relatives
    Who've found their loved ones slayed
    It prevents retaliation
    Gives the buck a place to stop
    And allows the better-financed
    To dodge the harm they'd cop
    And so they happ'ly stabbed and shot
    And battered, biffed and bit
    Unsheathing family relics
    To ensure that throats were slit
    A blade was deemed the choicest tool
    When it came to settling scores
    It has finesse and it has elegance
    With a flick it'll drop your drawers
    The Aussies were quite famous
    For slashing north and east and west
    Even southward got a look-in
    As they showed whose clan was best
    For the Aussies were divided
    Into groups that numbered a dozen
    Each ably representing

A hierarchy of cousins
Every family had a hat it wore
To proclaim its own upstanding,
Emblazoned with a coats of arms:
A most-distinctive branding

This is an example of a
hat worn by an Australian.

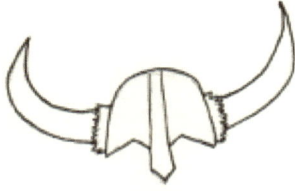

So too is this.

The group to which young Ted belonged
Was the one by name of Kelly
He fit within its lower ranks
At about the height of belly
This was owing to his status
As a child deprived of father
Let's take some time to focus on
And explain the whole palaver.

TED'S HISTORY:

Ted's Old Man left the planet
    Prior to Ted's arrival here
    It happened on a business trip
    'Twas an illness quite severe
    It claimed him with alacrity
    He was buried beneath the earth
    His mates all raised their glasses
    And remarked upon his worth

Ted's mother passed Ted over
To a lady name of Ruby
'Twas her job to raise him rightly
With the aid of her right booby.

The left one was reserved in full
    For the offspring all her own
    She had six or seven or maybe ten
    Some were even fully grown
    Nanna Rube as she was mainly known
    Was a wet nurse by profession
    Stoic in her temperament
    And known for self-possession

She took young Ted out to the wild
To live among her tribe
Tough and wiry quick and strong
On himself he soon relied
Rube's people lived in wurlie huts
And rode round on megafauna
Ted's siblings all were indigenes
He had a sister named Big Lorna
Ted was with this rugged crew
When battered by the news
His mum had died on holidays
On a quest to get new shoes

The locale was Wangaratta
    A place we'll hear of more
    They blamed an influenza
    Said it pushed her out the door
    The funeral was a quiet event
    But classy all the same
    Ted rose and gave a eulogy
    Making pure his mother's name
    And afterwards he found himself
    In the care of an uncle proper
    The brother of his father
    Uncle Harry the Lady Dropper

He was a batchelor, good ol' Hazza
    He would never keep 'em round
    Not when they kept on talking
    Or singing, or making sound
    He took young Ted beneath his wing
    And told him he was callow
    'But never mind, young Teddy boy
    'You're a soil that still is fallow.
    'I've got some things to teach you, mate
    'Y'can learn the family trade
    'And I guarantee that if ya learn it well
    'You'll find your life is made.'
    Harry was a trader
    And he showed young Ted the ropes:
    How to strike a cunning deal
    And avoid the death of hopes

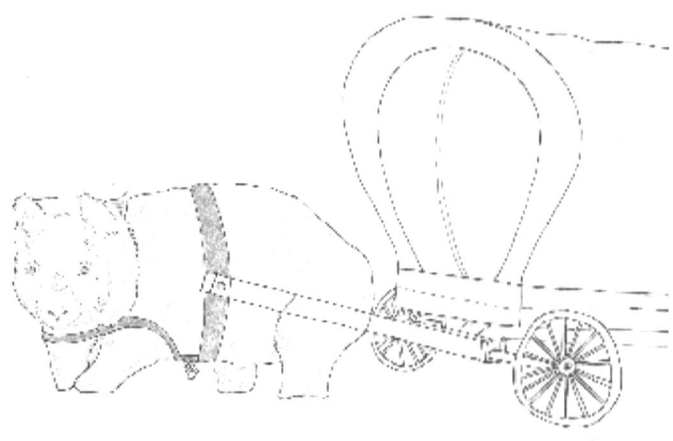

"Cause the secret here young Teddy boy
    'Is to never let 'em know
    'The depths of your desperation
    'How low you're prepared to go.'
    As the years began to trundle by
    Ted grew from boy to teen
    Then adolescent to full grown-up
    A trader skilled and clean

His prowess is what caught the eyes
　　Of a wealthy chook named Beryl
　　When first they traded pleasantries
　　She thought, *My he's far from feral*

Beryl

She liked his hard-work ethic
And his honesty to boot
And because she was a widow
She thought his youth was mighty cute
She popped the marital question
On his birthday twenty-five
Saying, 'Be ye not so flattered
'I'm barely just alive.' *
*Beryl was forty.
'Come on Bez,' he then replied
'Enough with that sorta speak
'I look at you and I think *phwoar*
'*Ma knees are goin weak.*'
With intention they got married
And with happiness spent their hours
Drinking tea and breeding poodles

Baking scones and sniffing flowers
But then there was a seismic shift
In their calm suburban life
Reality as they knew it
Was dipped head-first into strife.

THE FIRST VISITATION

On a fateful and now-famous day
    Ted sought some solitude
    In a rustic mountain man-cave
    Where he often stripped off nude
    Was he naked in that crucial hour?
    No historian can say for sure
    But they always note the awesome power
    That drove him to the floor.
    'AAAAAAAAAHHHHHHHHH!!!!!!!!!' is what he said at first
    When the Angel showed his face
    He said his name was Ferdinand
    And he moved with style and grace
    With coiffed blonde hair and a robe most pale
    And a grin of shining ivory
    Ferdy, as he called himself
    Was smugly cloaked in livery.

Their initial interaction
Was rough, to say the least
Ted thought the Angel Ferdy
Was in fact demonic beast*
*Aka bunyip.
And so he tried to kill himself
By leaping off a mountain
But Ferdy came and stopped him
And then began a'shoutin:
'I am a representative
'Of the Bloke Who Lives Upstairs
'Allan is his formal name
'He deserves both pomp and airs
'Those more close-acquainted
'Call him Al in reverent tone
'Big Al would be the safest
'To ensure respect is shown.

'Big Al has got a mission
'For you there, Mr Kell
'To send you out across the land
'With a product you must sell.
'*The True Blue Way* is its formal name
'It's an ethos from on high
'A way of life so magical
'It has come from out the sky.
'With phrases known as *quotables*
'(These are pithy little grabs)
'You'll speak of Big Al's wisdom
'And his plans for keeping tabs –
'On all the people of the earth
'Who are ratbags and ill-bred;
'Who are heading for a fiery realm
'If they flout these words I've said.
'The name for such is *Mongrel*
'And they're called this for a reason
'Their thoughts are wicked nasty ones
'Filled with lust and hate and treason
'The treason that I speak of
'Is the fact that they don't comply
'With the True Blue Way of Doing Things
'The ethos from the sky
'Hence you must reveal their ways
'Are wayward, Mr Kelly
'For in not long the earth will shake
'And quiver like it's jelly
'I'm referring to a certain day
'*Judgment* is its name
'It's appeared on the horizon
'Soon all will feel its flame.'
Ted scampered home and told his wife
Of all these things to be
Of Judgment Day and Big Al's wrath

And Mongrels blind to see
Bez listened most attentively
And let him speak his mind
Then cleared her throat and said she thought
It's time her name was signed –
On the dotted line that did decree
One's True Blue membership
And with that declaration
Member One Hoorayed Hip Hip!

MEMBER NUMBER TWO

The second convert to the Way
    Was a nephew name of Frederick
    Ted and Beryl had adopted him
    When the country became drought strick

    Freddy, as he called himself
    Was a quiet and tidy lad
    Always with a happy grin
    And rarely feeling sad
    Only ten when signing name
    On the True Blue Members page
    Fred proved a loyal follower

Was devoted till old age.

WAGGA WAGGA WAGGA...
WAGGA WAGGA

Wagga Wagga Wagga
    The town where Ted first spoke
    Is short for a much longer name
    Two more Waggas one must croak
    But a drawn-out way of phrasing
    The title of one's town
    Proved a hassle and a hardship
    So the Aussies chipped it down
    Wagga, as they called it
    Was a town of team and trade
    Where the canny and ambitious
    Could find their dreams get made
    Of course there always was the risk
    Of absorbing blade or buckshot
    But knowing the right people
    Holds at bay the often'd mugshot
    Ted was well protected
    By family connections;
    Uncle Harry (who had raised him)
    Was a man held in affection –
    By the many varied citizens
    Who comprised the Waggan clans
    They doffed their hats in passing
    To show how Hazza stands
    But the reach of their toleration
    Was tested thence by Ted
    Whose maiden declarations
    Made their Waggan faces red
    Ted built himself a soapbox

And took it into town
Then stepped atop his podium
And made a *heht-hem* sound

Naturally no one listened
They were all too deep absorbed
In the process known as barracking
For the teams they each adored
See the Aussies were a sporting breed
With a fixed and firm tradition
Of gathering at a certain place
To hold forth with erudition
They each avowed their Bloke Upstairs
Was the fella to admire
So at the Pub they hunkered down
And cheered his name up higher

Unruly was the outcome
As these yelling teams competed
To have their cherished Man Above
Hold the mantle Undefeated
And likely was it difficult
To gauge the Bloke on top
Unless one's fella in the sky
Hapt to bless one's crop
Ted Kelly was persistent
He cleared his throat some more
And cast his True Blue message
Above the barracking roar
'The sky is gonna rip in half!
'The seas'll boil away!
'Mountains'll shake to powder!
'And the dead'll leave their grave!
'Everyone'll end up naked!
'In Group A or in Group B!
'There'll be Mongrels in the former!
'They'll miss out on the Big P!
'*Paradise* is what I'm speaking of!
'It's the place ya wanna be!

'It's the joint where drinks are always cold!
'Served by virgins (seventy-three)!
'The other place is torturous!
'Infinitely so!
'The name is Hell and can't you tell!
'You do not wanna go –
'To this horrid place of scorching flames!
'Where ya drink hot scalding water!
'And eat pus and thorns and have your skin!
'Ripped off daily, cooked to order!

'Now brace yourselves for bombshells!
    'I do not wanna say it!
    'But the message Al has given me!
    'Can*not* be un-convey'd!
    'Your ancestors are writhing now!
    'In that evil place called Hell!
    'They did not live the True Blue Way!
    'There's nothing more to tell!

'The fruits that they're all eating!
'Look like snake heads, yes indeed!
'The tree from which they amply sprout!
'Grew from Stannie's planted seed!
'But don't worry, I'm here to tell you!
'Y'can dodge that sickly meal!
'If ya listen to my warning!
'With joy you'll surely squeal!
'For the plans that Big Al has in store!
'For the people of this earth!
'Are grand in scope and nature!
'And they ring with shiny worth!'
Was Ted surprised when offal flew
In response to these huge claims
That dearly-parted loved ones
Were all living in the flames?
Did he falter when he spoke up loud
To make the fact well known
That he now possessed a business card
With occupation fully shown?

Ted Kelly's business card.
1st edition. Registered Prognosticator
Courtesy of True Blue Heritage Collection.

Prognosticating Spokesman
Was the title he adopted
Or rather it was given him
By Big Al, who had co-opted –

And welcomed Ted into the fold
The Club of True Blue Kind
Ted was deemed its captain
Big Al the guiding mind
'Cause Ted was Big Al's mouthpiece
The man to lead his Team
A Team with only three decrees
To summarise its dream
1) There is no Bloke but Allan
Upstairs above the sky
2) And Ted's his final spokesman
3) So perfect one could cry
Those three decrees were poorly met
That hot historic day
When Ted addressed the Waggans
Beginning with *G'day*
He catalysed some whispers
Some gossip and some strife
Then wandered home oblivious
To have dinner with his wife.

CANBRUSALEM

In the city of Canbrusalem
    Established long ago
    There were two kinds of peoples
    Of both ye shall now know
    The people called Jazoozites
    Had very peculiar ways
    They liked to keep among themselves
    And didn't like to graze –
    With sheep that came from other flocks
    Or goats with vacant eyes
    People not Jazoozites
    Were people who told lies
    Jazoozites were responsible
    For another kind of folk
    Christophites is the name they take
    To commemorate a bloke –
    Who claimed to have descended from
    A place among the clouds
    To walk the earth and roam about
    Singing songs and building crowds
    The 'Zoozites found a trebuchet
    And put Christoph upon it
    They launched him back up to the sky
    With a wave and quoted sonnet

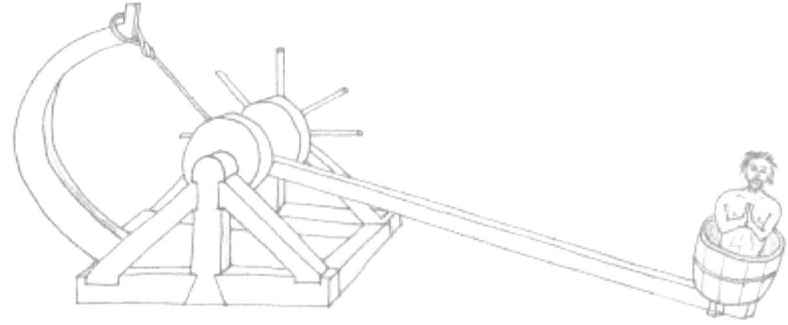

The cunning plan was ably hatched
By Jazoozite patriarchy
Who didn't much like Christophites
And their raving mad malarkey
They flung the pesky irritant
And wiped their hands of that
Thinking this would be the end of it
Christoph hopes were flat

eye-witness rendering
of the incident.

But this in fact was not the case
The Christophites all were hopeful
That in good time their man above
Would drop them down a ropeful –
And lift them all up to the sky
To live their days out there

Eating toast and drinking lemonade
Lying back without a care
The Jazoozites and the Christophites
With their differing perspectives
Are notably divergent
In their earthly-life objectives
Jazoozites say to make amends
For the ratbag things you do
Christophites say that *Chris* did that
There's nothing *left* to do
They both possess entitlement
To a long prestigious line
Of Prognosticating Spokesmen
Who were tellers of their time
Hearing daily from their Bloke Above
They'd give a firm report
Of trends and demographics
And ways of falling short
Christoph, some said, was meant to be
The primo of this kind
And although he was Jazoozite
Jazoozite teeth did grind –
In response to the assertion
That Christoph was meant to rout
The ones who kept Canbrusalem
From the hands of banded lout.

THE BRITONS

The Britons came from Britain
    A city far away
    They set up shop and smacked some bots
    Prompting 'Zoozites all to say –
    'Ya got no right to be here!
    'But your cannons let ya stay!
    'One day there'll be uprising!
    'Jazoozite be the way!'
    Until that day there was no choice

But to stomach status quo
Jazoozites shrugged and paid the tax
Let the Britons run the show

This occurred within Canbrusalem
Where 'Zoozites long had dwelled
Till the Britons had a gutful
And had its buildings shelled
The place was all but levelled
When the Brits were finally through
They even burned the clubhouse
The pride of all Jazoo

The 'Zoozites quickly realised
There was little left to do
They packed their bags and hit the road
Saying Bye to Canny Brue.

1 + 1 + 1 = TED

'Zoos headed out across the lands
    To many different nations
    Raising tents and plying trades
    Performing tip castrations
    They had themselves a certain way
    Of marking out their breed
    They'd grab a knife and cut the prong
    Of a baby that it bleed
    The Christophites did not do this
    They'd left that rite behind
    But they were just as quirky:
    They tried to cure the blind
    The 'Zoo and Christophite disagreements
    Rolled often across the land
    Churning such discussion
    That many did understand –
    The general disposition
    Of each respective team
    And where a thread might zoom away
    To effect unstitch'd seam.
    Some say Ted heard these stories
    On his business trips away
    And decided he could use them
    To enrich the True Blue Way
    But Ted would say that *Ferdinand*
    Was the source of all his speech
    His words all came from Big Al's mouth
    So with fervour did he preach –
    That 'Zoo and Christophite handbooks
    Had their stories all round wrong
    And at the top of all their sagas
    There did *Ted* belong!

Mr Kelly was the hero
They'd all been waiting for
He'd lead the merry way Upstairs
To party ever more.
To cultivate a middle ground
To show his loving heart
Ted said the 'Zoos and Christophites
Could keep their tales and art
They were fine to keep their stories
Till the narratives got to Ted
But from there it was essential
That everybody said –
Big Al's the only Bloke Upstairs
And Ted's his representative
You cannot get a better sort
Let's be friends, not argumentative
The first time all of this was said
Some did not quite agree
With Teddy's fresh perspectives
And his new theology
Jazoozites said, *Yeah righto mate*
No worries, enjoy yourself
Christophites said, *That's interesting*
Not for us, but go in health
Ted turned away upon that day
With letters of rejection
But did not throw his pamphlets
Of membership selection
The True Blue Way was sure to grip
On the day it needed to
The people of Australia
Would see it all was true
They'd doff their hats toward Big Al
They'd barrack for his Team
Their every conversation

Would centre on the theme –
Of how Big Al was peerless
There was none who could compare
And Ted, who represented him
Should flamin' run for mayor.

CAPTAIN ABRAHAM HAD MANY SONS

MANY SONS HAD CAPTAIN ABRAHAM

If in case you're wondering
   From whence Jazoozites came
   A Captain name of Abraham
   First stamped the family name

He'd set out with a merry crew
Hauling chests and paraphernalia
Intrepid in his noble hope
Of travelling Australia
The intention of his journey
Was to find a quiet spot
Where he and several girl-friends
Could keep writing *Who Begot*
At a certain point he sired a kid
Then another came along
The appearance of the runner-up
Is where things all turn'd wrong
A case of acrimony
Made the Captain raise his boot
And plant it to the backside
Of his elder loinal fruit
The young man who was but a teen
Was volleyed out of home
With him went his mother
Surely seething spit and foam
They wandered off into the scrub
And learned to hunt and gather
The young man grew into a bloke
Who had no time for blabber
Rough as guts and wild of eye
Scruffy as is possible
One wouldn't put it past him:
He formed views on who was robbable
As well as that he had some fun
Out from him flowed descendants
They're now all known as Aussies
Yes they're commonly defendants.
But such facts are a digression
From the point that one was making
The *younger* son of Captain Abe

Is why now the ground is shaking
For from that humble runner-up
A different tribe had grown
Branded in its psyche is:
Jazoozite to the bone.

BACK TO THE WAG (pronounced WOG)

Haemo-cash was offered
    As a price for Ted Kell's head
    On account of all the horrid things
    He'd said about the dead
    The Waggans could not handle
    Ted's ill-begotten claim
    (Wholly un-retracted)
    That dead relatives live in flame
    So they visited Ted's uncle
    Harry, the Lady Dropper
    And said, 'Oi Haz your nephew
    'He's gonna come a cropper –
    'If ya fail to put a muzzle on
    'His cheeky sneaky gob
    'We simply cannot stomach it
    'We'll *have* to do the job
    'His comments are uncalled for
    'Would you give us the permission
    'To quietly sweep him off the earth
    'Wanna sniff this here commission?'
    Harry smelled the cash and sighed
    Saying, 'Sorry, cannot do it
    'He's me brother's one and only kid
    'If ya offed 'im, I would rue it.'
    The Aussies they all turned away
    With their clean respective hats
    But vowed to find another way
    Of exacting This for Thats.

DOWN AT THE PUB

Apparently, the story goes
    The Pub where Aussies gather
    Was built by Captain Abraham
    But that might be simply blather
    Regardless, they believe it
    The Aussies at the Pub
    Who go down there to barrack
    And serve other teams a drub
    Ted found the nerve to wander down
    His soapbox in his hands
    And give a speech that no one liked
    Thinking *Al, got other plans?'*
    He had not heard from Ferdinand
    For a goodly decent while
    That the Angel was ignoring him
    Made Teddy lose his smile
    And the Waggans were contemptuous
    Of the good ol' True Blue Way
    They all believed it bulldust
    Nothing positive did they say
    Ted found this quite disheartening
    Dispiriting, in fact
    Perhaps he'd just gone crazy
    Perhaps his mind had cracked
    'Cause who on earth sees Angels
    'When they're sittin' in a cave?
    'Just the big-eyed dreadlocked types
    'Who cough and spit and rave.'
    Ted kicked the dust and wandered home
    Hoping Bez might rub his feet
    When suddenly there was Ferdinand
    Floating high above the street.

'Ferdy ya flamin' boof head!'
Shouted Ted with bouncing glee
'Where the flamin' hell ya been
'No doubt ignoring me!'
'Sorry Ted,' said Ferdinand
'I'm flat out off ma feet
'Ya would not bloomin' credit
'The crews I've had to meet
'But that's all now behind us
'So listen here real close
'I've got some things to teach you
'It'll help ya learn the ropes.'

THE HEAD BOB

'See everybody doffs the hat
    'Or pumps a skyward fist
    'To make sure that their Bloke Above
    'Can feel his bum is kissed
    'But the proper way to do it
    'I shall here and now display
    'It'll change your life entirely
    'And ignite the True Blue Way
    'I completely guarantee you
    'That when this fire takes hold
    'It'll spread so fast there will not last
    'Any memory of the cold
    'Stand tall with both your shoulders back
    'And stretch your neck up high
    'Then tilt your head toward the ground
    'In defiance of the sky

'Now do all that repeatedly
    'As many times ya can
    'Big Al calls this the *head bob*
    'It's a part of his great plan.'
Ted gave a demonstration
On his soapbox at the Pub

He dipped his head right forward
To draw members to The Club
''Cause Big Al's Team is different
'To any other type
'And if anyone says otherwise
'On their back there'll be a stripe
'Big Al he does not muck around
'When it comes to Upstairs things
'Ya better bloody learn the words
'Of the anthem that he sings.'
True to what the Angel said
The head bob quick took hold
It spread throughout the Waggan crowd
Like a raging ravenous mould
At least until some necks got sore
And people voiced the view
The head bob was unhealthy
That much they knew was true
But Ted and Bez and nephew Fred
Soon found themselves allied
With Waggans who decided
With Big Al's Team they'd side
Defying persecution
Calling themselves True Blue
They made habit of the head bob
These members fresh and new.

EARLY TEAM-MATES

Hamish was a beefy bloke
    With a mouth foul like a dunny
    He was built like one and had a smile
    That lit up bright and sunny

Hamish

He joined the Way one afternoon
    On return from hunting geese
    This biggest man in Wagga
    With a beard like ragged fleece
    Hame stuck his face in that of Mick

Who apparently was hassling Ted
Saying, 'Oi Mick ya stinkin' mongrel
'Leave him 'lone is what I said.'
He struck old Mick with the butted end
Of his shotgun (name of Bruce)
And said if Mick did not relent
He'd blast his pale caboose
Mick said, 'Yeht, no worries, Hame.
'I'll leave ol' Ted alone
'Tell him sorry for chuckin' eggs at him
'That's not behaviour fully grown.'
Hamish naturally satisfied
Let go of young Mick's throat
And told him that he might be wise
To step on Big Al's boat.
Another early convert
To the growing Kelly Gang
Was a bloke who said his name was Wayne
Then followed that with slang

Formerly he had spent much time
    Picking fights with Kellyites
    He'd even thumped his sister
    When she'd prattled off some sound bytes
    But a sudden change of heart ensued
    And Wayne became True Blue
    His love for Ted and Big Al's Team
    Well, it grew and grew
    On the day he joined the Gang
    He knocked on Ted's front door
    Saying, 'Ted I'm here right with ya
    'Ya need not ask for more.'
    This was good for Ted to hear
    Due to recent Wag events
    Some Aussies had got together
    To give voice to their offence
    They nailed their stipulations
    To the front door of the Pub

Saying Wags can't trade with Kellyites
And maritally they can't rub
Could an insult be much bigger
Ted didn't think it could
He was at heart a Waggan
His intentions all were good
But the aggro aimed at Kellyites
Was becoming so outrageous
That he'd told some of his followers
To leave Wagga, it's too dangerous
They left and Teddy stayed behind
With a handful of his crew
These remnants looked toward him
Sure that *he'd* know what to do
Ted said, 'Big Al won't let us down
'He's behind us good and proper
'And don't worry none'll kill me
'Thanks to Haz the Lady Dropper.'
But Haz was old and running fast
Toward life's finish line
Ted knew that soon there'd come a day
He'd plumb an empty mine
But till that day the True Blue Way
Would yes be spouted bold
''Cause all of us are Kellyites
'And no we won't be told –
'The way by which to barrack
'Or tilt our bobbin' noggins
'Big Al's the one who says what's what
''Ken Oath it's not the Waggans!'

UNCLE BARRY

Around about this general time
    Ted's other uncle, Barry
    Was walking down a crowded road
    And trying not to tarry
    When he looked across and saw a man
    Laid flat beneath a rock.
    A slave by name of Leroy
    Was going into shock

So too was Uncle Barry
Who looked at Leroy's owner
Saying, 'Oi ya bloody scurvy dog
'Has he given you pneumonia?
'Why would ya treat a man like that?
'It's nasty all the way
'Get that rock from off his chest
'Or I'll have more to say.'
'Hey aren't you sir a Kellyite?'
Said the owner to Uncle Baz
'If that's the case then listen here
'You're the reason this bloke has –
'A bloated rock on top his form
'He says he's one of you
'And that good sir I'm sad to say
'Is not the thing to do.'
In a short amount of time they struck
A deal between each other
Barry would buy Leroy
For a sum that pleased his mother*
* *That is, Leroy's mother.*
Leroy in some latter days

Was the first to sing the song
That Ferdy gave to Captain Kell
So True Blues could sing along –
To a hymn that is their very own
It makes their values understood
But we'll get to that in days to come
In a different neighbourhood.
Heading back to Barry
We'll give the man his dues
'Cause if it were not for him
There'd be no Truly Blues
Harry had a pair of lungs
Which were born to gain attention
And he used them in the early days
To gain some crowd retention
Bazza cranked the limelight
When Teddy, scared to speak
Was hiding behind his soapbox
Looking pale and awful meek
At first it was an irritant
That bloody Uncle Baz
Had turned the spotlight on him
In a state of Nervous As
But Ted grew ever comfortable
And soon he was a'cryin'
The niceties that Kellyites
Will tell ya when they're lyin'.

THE NICE'TIES AND NAS'TIES

There are some things a Kellyite
    Will say to ease one's mind
    They do it so a Mongrel
    Might remain content and blind
    Ted Kelly was quite generous
    In his first ten years of teaching
    And to this mass of quotables
    Is where Kellyites are reaching –
    When they wish to throw a thickly rug
    'Twixt clapper and warning bell
    That a person most suspicious
    Might decide there's nought to smell
    "There's no compulsion when it comes to teams,"
    Is the quote they often say
    (Though the history soon to follow
    (Might suggest that's not the way)
    "Feed the poor, treat strangers well,"
    And this they surely do
    (Provided the poor are Kellyites
    Irredeemably True Blue).
    And one suspects the "strangers"
    Are Mongrels in their make up
    Who if they learned how they were viewed
    Would receiveth quite a wake up.
    For the nice'ties are used to hide
    The nas'ties, y'see
    Fibbing, they do call this
    Even do it doctrinally
    Focus on some minuscules
    Ignore the larger picture
    See it's just a misconception
    There is nasty in our mixture

Abundant is the literature
That describes this common ploy
Elsewhere shall ye find it
Please do – you will enjoy!*
Enjoy might not be the correct term.

FAMILY FRICTIONS

Somebody grabbed a jawbone
    And cracked a Kellyite
    Who lost a tooth and split his lip
    And got an awful fright
    'Cause Ted had called a meeting
    Asking Waggans to attend
    Forty of them gathered
    To hear their former friend
    Ted told them that their merry ways
    Were sending them to Hell
    And said, 'Oi you mob listen
    'You're Mongrels, can't you tell?
    'There is no better message
    'Than the one that Big Al sends
    'Sign your name, become True Blue
    'And then we'll all be friends!'
    Freddy at this time was twelve
    He stood up on his feet
    And said in front of everyone,
    'This message can't be beat!
    'I'm with ya, Ted, this golden path
    'Holds adventure to be sure.'
    The Waggans laughed their heads off
    Then stood and used the door
    Uncle Barry ambled over
    Put a hand on Teddy's shoulder
    'Come on mate, let's not be late
    'Uncle Hazza's gettin' colder.'
    Uncle Harry in his ancient state
    Was lying on his bed
    Thinking often of the land above
    Which he'd roam when labelled dead

He called young Teddy to him
And said, 'Now listen mate
'Why don't ya lift the handbrake
''Fore you're buried under slate
'All me neighbours have admitted
'A grudging admiration
'The way ya coin a phrase they say
'Is magic, no protestation
'But even *that* is dangerous
''Cause some went on to say
'You are in fact a sorcerer
'You're makin' hair go grey
'Be careful, Ted, that's all I'll say
'I've heard of a committee
'The Waggans did assemble
'To make your name un-pretty
'They reckon that the tourists
'Are askin' after you
'Apparently the True Blue Way
'Tastes good as kangaroo
'They ask where they can find you
'Where you'll plant the famous soap box
'And if anybody sells your face
'Embroidered on some new socks

'But beware that delegation
'That's what I'm tryin' to say
'The Waggans are a crafty lot
'With them one should not play.'
Dying Hazza had confirmed it:
Ted Kelly's star was rising
But only in the lands beyond
Which was hardly thought surprising
In Wagga Ted was still a man
Regarded with disdain
And though he tried to hide it
The insults caused him pain
'Specially when an aunty
(The wife of Uncle *Larry*)
Said Ted was just a layabout
Whom one would never marry
She didn't like Ted's epic tales
(Which he'd borrowed from Jazoozites)
These new improved adventures
Were hardly filled with insights
And the fact that Ted quite often said
That other Blokes Upstairs
Were kruddy frail and paltry

Weighed greatly on her cares
In fact one day this aunty
Set out to lay a trap
On account of Ted's assertions
That other teams were crap
She wandered out collecting thorns
Then laid them at Ted's door
And waited with great eagerness
For the howl of pain that swore
As well as that there came a curse
From under Ted's tin hood
That the wife of Uncle Larry
Would have hands as dead as wood
And she'd quickly take a downward trip
On a pilgrimage to Hell
Uncle Laz was rich but he'd go too
They'd both enjoy the smell.

NEEDLESS TO SAY

The rhetoric of Ted Kelly
    Had embraced a darkened quality
    No longer did he gently say
    That all should join his polity
    Where before he might have said things
    In a tone with tact and charm
    Now he did not give a rip
    If he tore off leg and arm
    His followers were duly tasked
    The job of smash-and-grabbing
    The trinkets and the artefacts
    Of teams that needed jabbing
    'Cause heretofore resistance
    Was afforded toleration
    But now it was regarded
    The food for indignation
    'Get hold their scarves and grab their flags
    'And chuck 'em down a hole
    'If there's pictures of their Blokes Upstairs
    'Smash 'em, that's the goal
    ''Cause this right here's the difference
    ''Tween us and stupid others
    '*Al* cannot be photographed
    'He's a man devoid of brothers
    'If any say they know Al's face
    'They're lying straight to yours
    'Only Al sees his reflection
    'Dis-heed those flapping maws!'

NATURALLY

The town of Wag erupted
    With chaos and with strife
    Threats were bandied left and right
    In regard to ending life.

STAN'S QUOTABLES

Hamish, Wayne and Uncle Baz
    Were always 'longside Ted
    Without this bulky entourage
    He'd surely end up dead.
    They stopped a delegation
    As it trod to have word
    Quietly with Captain Ted
    Whose wrath was then deferred
    These humble representatives
    Of peace-desiring Waggans
    Had drafted a proposal
    To avoid more needless floggins
    'What say this, Ted, a compromise
    'A meeting 'bout halfway?
    'What if all us Waggans
    'Embrace the bob today?
    'If *we* agree to nod our heads
    'In time with Big Al's crew
    'Will *you* all maybe have a go
    'To see if *ours* is true?
    ''Cause we've all got a theory
    'Relating straight to method
    'The bestest way of barracking
    'Will be announced with little effort.'

Ted's first response was, 'Never!'
But then he changed his mind
And said, 'Yeah righto you blokes
'Head bob all in time!'
A joint communal gathering
Took place at the usual spot
Where people all inclined their heads
To sort out what was not –
The bestest way of barracking
'Cause then it would be evident
Which method was the one to call
A dear and welcomed resident.
The details of the episode
Are that Waggans bobbed the head
Toward three Upstairs sheilas
Representing Al, 'twas said
Ferdy heard about it
And swooped in mighty quick
Shouting, 'Ted what are ya doing?!'
And gave his head a flick

'Don't ya know there's only Al
'The others are all fake
'Three-hundred-sixty-*plus*-of-em!
'Hoh, for goodness sake!
'Go and grab your soapbox
'And put yourself upon it
'Make clear the engine problems
'Takin' place beneath your bonnet
'Ol' Stan he has put bulldust
'Across your flamin' pupils
'It's resulted in your followers
'Behavin' without scruples.'
Ted evidently looked about
And gauged this was the case
'Cause next thing he was shouting loud
With a strained and reddened face:
'I'm taking back entirely
'All what I said before
'The members of the True Blue Way
'Shall be mixed up nevermore!
'We do not share our head bob
'With any other team
'If any try to force it
'Engage 'em with a scream
'Yours or theirs it matters not
'Long as message makes it through
'We abide by certain protocols
'That's why we're called True Blue!'
The going-back on what-he'd-said
Apparently makes the case
That Ted was not quite perfect
As he claimed with straightened face
But onward went the Captain
He gave a dissertation
In which he broadly outlined

The origins of Satan

'Stanley is a cheeky bloke
'Angelic in his features
'Got booted out of heaven
''Cause of us here mortal creatures
'See Big Al made us out of clay
'And set us up real straight

'But Stannie wouldn't toe the line
'Refused to get prostrate
'See he's behind the All-of-It
'He's down here runnin' round
'Here on earth, where he spends his time
'Lurin' people underground
'He's fibbed to *all* the Spokesman
'So all o' this is natural
'Let it not distract us
'We can't think multi-lateral
'And while we're on that subject
'I've one more thing to say
'About the fiery torment
'For those who spurn The Way
'Woe to the vain and privileged
'Hell's waiting for your kind
'Your possessions will not save you
'From the horrors you will find –
'Way down in Hell where do abide
'The sinful, deaf and blind;
'All who shoulda looked more hard
'For Big Al's fluro signs!

BIG AL'S FLURO SIGNS

Stars and rain, and night and day
And ships with useful stuff
Are focal points of gratitude
They should never make ya gruff
Life-giving rains and changing winds
And iron with strength of war
Are classed as further of evidence
Of Big Al's guiding paw
And cow milk that is tasty
And bees 'cause they eat fruit
And don't forget the honey
They quick and ably shoot
That stuff is therapeutic
Real good for pain'd guts
If people can't connect the dots
Frankly ma'am, they're nuts.

DADDY IGNORAMUS

If any man is thought to be
    The unredeem'd nemesis of Ted
    It's a bloke whose lengthy title
    Starts eagerly with *Fred*
    We'll know him by another name
    Bestowed by the True Blue Captain
    Daddy Ignoramus
    Is the title he's now wrapped in.
    He'd often read the paper
    And learn what Ted was doing
    Mutter to himself and think,
    My this fly needs shooing
    Ted was causing trouble

Even simpletons could see
And without intervention
Residents soon would flee
They'd take their cash from out of town
So too would go their skills
The Wag would be a sickly joint
Deprived of needed pills
It was Daddy I who called the meet
That Haz had heard about
He'd got some Wags together
And plotted Ted Kell's rout

None was too enchanted
By the Kellyite incursion
And how Crawlers to the famous Pub*
Came back from their excursion –
*A Pub Crawler is an Australian who makes an annual pilgrimage to
Wagga's famous Pub.
With a sight of Ted the high point
Out of one's entire trip
What accounted for this fever

That had Aussies in its grip?
That tourists came from all around
Obviously was not bad
But to see ol' Captain Teddy?
Surely they were mad!
'And look, if they keep coming
'This riff-raff we can see
'In not too long our town'll be
'Reserved for mockery'
Ideas arose within the smoke
That poured from out cigars
Some were met with *Hmms*
And others conjured *Ahhhhs*
The brandy that was swilled in bulk
Inspired a many giggle
And a crafty plan that, said each man
'From this, Ted will not wriggle'
Haemo-cash was push'd forth
By a dozen representatives
Each declared a spokesman
For a family argumentative
But prior disagreements
Underwent subordination
That the clans might get together
With the goal of Ted's ablation
'Here's what we'll do,' said Daddy Ig
When the plot was halfway done
'We'll each employ a citizen
'To use a knife or gun
''Cause if every single entry point
'Is owed to a different man
'The blame that spurts from out the wounds
'Can't land on just one clan.'
'Mate, you are a genius,'
Said one of his tipsy peers

'This plan of ours is brilliant
'It'll have 'em on their rears.
'But oi we'd better hurry
''Cause you know what I've heard?
'Captain Kelly has a secretary
'He's writin' every word
'Every single quotable
'Is bein' jotted down
'Ted's knockin' up a book, he says
'The first one from our town.'
'Hang-on hang-on hang-on'
Said another of the men
'The statement you just uttered
'Right there it does not end
'I'm pretty sure that Wagga
'Is not alone in lack production
'It is in fact *Australia*
'Which is known for cultural suction.'
'You mean that this'll be the book
'That marks an Aussie first?
'Bloody hell we've gotta stop this
'This has gone from bad to worst
'If Ted becomes an author
'Then we're all buggered flat
'And the friendly town of Wagga
'Will be known as polished scat.'

HEADLINE -
A JOURNEY MOST UNPLANNED

Although the Aussies had no books
    They had a printing press
    And thanks to Wagga's goings-on
    It suffered much duress
    On the Wednesday of a certain year
    The Aussies woke and scanned
    A squib that had the title
    A Journey Most Unplanned
    Ted Kelly, who was interviewed
    Firmly did avow
    That several nights the previous
    He'd woken, screaming, '*Wow!*'
    A nudge upon his bunioned foot
    Had wrenched him from his sleep
    And revealed a giant creature
    Tall as wells are deep
    Propped upon the saddle
    Of this creature which had wings
    Was the Angel known as Ferdy
    Who remarked on several things
    'First of all don't try to class
    'This creature that you see
    'Is it possum, is it wombat?
    'Who knows, just let it be
    'Climb up here, my good friend Ted
    'You're going for a ride
    'It's time you got a decent glimpse
    'Of what's on the other side.'
    Ted climbed upon the saddle

On the giant rodent's back
Then held on tight in deathly fear
And cringed and screamed, *Alack!*
The creature lifted up its legs
Then jumped into the sky
Ted overcome his nerves and saw
Swiftly they did fly
Over rooftops, over streets
(Wooden-tiled and cobbled)
They rocketed, this man and beast
The latter most unhobbled
With every step the creature took
It drew the far horizon
Closer to its flying self
With Teddy screaming, *Scheissen!*

In briefest time Ted looked below
And saw an awesome sight
'Neath them was Canbrusalem
Asleep beneath the night
If all of that's not strange enough
This tale of flying beast
There's one more thing to comment on

Weird to say the least
They landed on the tiled roof
Of the biggest 'Zoozite clubhouse
(Never mind that it was levelled flat
(And eaten out by woodlouse
(The Britons they had knocked it down
(Five-hundred years the previous
(But the Captain, he said otherwise
('It was standing; just believe us.')
Dismounting with great elegance
Ted hopped down on the roof
Then had a conversation
With Jazoozites mighty couth
Prognosticating Spokesmen
(Of quite familiar name)
Had a chat with Teddy
And barracked without shame
Then a gleaming golden ladder
Rose up toward the sky
Ted began to climb it
Of course he said goodbye
He climbed up past the Gates of Hell
And snuck a peek inside
The things he saw beyond them
Can hardly be described
Unless one knows a language
Then easy it becomes
There were people eating burning coals
Which they pÜÜped from out their bums
And shelias who were strung up high
Hanging by their boobs
On account of "birthing bastards"
And spilling beans to rubes
Ted continued up to Heaven
Past a few more well-known chaps*

And found himself most greeted
With applause and high-five slaps
Former spokesmen.
On the seventh level skyward
There was a hefty mansion
And in it, Captain Abraham
On a throne of great expansion
Ted asked the Waggan journo
To grab the point real tight:
Seventy-thousand Angels
All make a daily flight –
To visit Captain Abraham
And step inside his house
Vowing not to leave it
Till a day considered grouse
That day relates to Judgment
When humans face the test
Take heed the signs before it:
Like a sunrise in the west
Remember that the Mongrels
All toddle off to Hell
And who goes up to Paradise?
The friends of Captain Kell
'But anyway Ted,' said Captain Abe
'Come meet a friend of yours
'His name'll be familiar
'It's been shot from many jaws.'
Ted probably dropped down on his face
At the point of introduction
The person he was meeting
Would have caused a mind eruption
When pressed for a description
Ted winced and wrung his hands
'A picture of Al's face,' he said
'Would violate Allan's plans

'But truly take it from me
'He's big and strong and tough
'And if ya make him grumpy
'Jeez he'll treat ya rough
'And this is what he told me
'As we chatted there together
'Traversing many subjects
'Like women, dogs and weather:
'"A good ole jolly head bob
'"Fifty times a day
'"Is the barrack I'm desiring
'"I've nothing more to say.'"
Thereafter soon departing
Ted skipped a-happy-way
And bumped into a bureaucrat
Who had some things to say
'Fifty sounds a fraction much
'Where head bobs are concerned
'I'd wander back to see Big Al
'Asking can his mind be turned?'
To shave a lengthy story down
And get right to the issue
Big Al picked up his edict
And tore it like mere tissue
The number fifty minimised
And became a single digit
'Surely five is not too much
'Could be done by *any* idjit.'
Those words were Al's and Ted agreed
That five was most delightful
He'd head on back to Wagga
So that Al could cop a sightful –
Of Team-mates bobbing heads real low
The movement done just right
Dawn and noon and *after*noon

Then sunset and the night
''Cause Big Al works like clockwork
'Like the sun and moon and stars
'He created all those systems
'Ya pack o' mad galahs
'And I betcha didn't know it:
'There's an old and ancient link
''Tween Al and that big shiny moon
'That paints your kitchen sink.'
The article waffled on some more
Slanting like a sinking ship
'Cause even back in those days
Journos couldn't tame the lip.
Its closing lines, per Ted's request
Made a mention quick and brief
Of how Captain Abe had said something
That stood out in relief:
Ted was now entitled to
The wife of an adopted son
Divorce would be in order
That's just the way things run.

RECEPTION

Many Waggans spat their orange juice
    Like the substance had gone bad
    Of course the general sentiment
    Was that Teddy had gone mad.
    But the supernatural journey
    Was a source of good publicity
    One might even say eventually
    Ted was treated with felicity.
    Caravans were loaded up
    People crawled toward the Pub
    When they couldn't find an outhouse
    They laid cable in the scrub
    Similar tales of hardship
    Were told around campfires
    By people fast becoming
    Official Ted admirers.
    Daddy Ignoramus,
    Aghast at such stupidity
    Got quickly on the blower
    And relayed with great rapidity –
    The need to solve the problem
    The one caused by Ted Kelly
    'We've got our twelve assassins
    'Representing every rellie
    'Tell 'em that our plan's on track
    'And when our strike is made
    'It's gonna be a deathly blow
    'To our friend Ted Kelly's trade.'

TO QUALIFY

It wasn't just Ted's influence
    Arousing great concern
    But his attitude most militant
    Best described as *Join or burn*
    A potential explanation
    For Ted Kelly's tonal swing
    Is found amid bereavements
    And the feelings that they bring
    Uncle Harry lost the citizenship
    That kept him on the earth
    And so did lovely Beryl
    A wife of highest worth

    Without the first Ted found himself
    Stripped of all protection
    And without the second he was said to be
    A man who'd lost direction
    Beryl was his bestest friend
    And when her soul went yonder

Some reckon that Ted Kelly's mind
Wheeled round and cleaved asunder
This is why the soapbox
Felt stomps and kicks and stamps
And Ted Kelly's pointed finger
Aimed straight at other camps
"Cause don'tcha know ya turkeys
'That Big Al's watchin' you
'And if ya do not join his Team
'He'll bash ya black and blue
'The fact that you'z all doff your hats
'Instead o' bobbin heads
'To Al is far more grievous
'Than any blood that sheds
'But if you Mongrels mend your ways
'Big Al is most forgiving
'But if you don't, well, frankly
'Your lives are not worth living.
'Fight for Al and Big Al's sake
"Gainst those who are against 'im
'Slay 'em where ya find 'em
'Subvert 'em till they're fenced in
'We'll set up leaders in the land
'And don't you think we won't
'The world'll end when True Blue rules
'Jot *that* down as a quote.'

THE ASSASSINS

'Have ya heard that flamin' Kellyites
　　'Have been breakin' into homes
　　'And smashin' paraphernalia:
　　'Collector mugs and even gnomes?

Examples of
team Paraphenalia

　　'They even killed somebody's dog
　　'A bloody Maltese shiatsu
　　'Tied it to a figurine
　　'Goodness, what did *it* do?
　　'See this deserves a discount
　　'We'll knock 'im at half price
　　'Let's head out now and stab the grub
　　'We'll lay 'im out on ice.'

THE ASSASSINATION

Ted was entertaining
   The night the killers struck
He had himself some visitors:
   A Wangarattan ruck
The men had all put on their shoes
   And left their doting wives
Convinced their noble mission
   Was the best one of their lives
They'd heard of Ted and things he'd said*
   Of course they were impressed;
When they rapped upon his wooden door
   In their finest they were dressed
*The nice'ties, as opposed to the nas'ties.
They told him they had made the trek
   To pop a solemn question:
Would Ted consider moving
   And gain the Wang's affection?
The town of Wangaratta
   (Obviously Wang for short)
Was currently filled with conflict
   Of a biffing-bashing sort
The Wangers needed someone
   To settle their disputes
The mentioned role of "arbiter"
   Let loose approving hoots.
Ted told them that he'd think about
   Their generous proposal
Then said goodnight, turned out the lights
   Flashed the neighbours with a robe pull
To the outside eye he went to bed
   But to those with clearer sight
He battened down the hatches

And got ready for a fight.
None can truly say for sure
How Ted learned of the plan
Some believe the plotting
Was heard while on the can
Wagga's public dunnies
Are a source of many whispers
The background noise is loud enough
It emboldens even lispers
Some think the scheme was overhead
By good ol' nephew Freddy
Who raced home quick and jumped in bed
Playin' ruse that he was Teddy
But this would mean the killers came
And had a fight with Fred
If that's what really happened, well
Fred would have wound up dead
But Freddy lived on after that
For days and weeks and years
He killed a many Mongrel
And abstained from many beers
'Cause Ted did not like alcohol
(Its effect upon the head)
So he spat in its direction
Drank apple juice instead.
Certainly he was sober
On that consequential night
He made it out adeptly
Perhaps by marring sight
Varying accounts attest
To different playings-out
In one the Angel Ferdy
Gave off a warning shout
Another says Ted wandered out
And blew a puff of bone dust

It blinded his attackers
And please'd Big Al utmost
Another says a stranger
Asked the killers about their business
Then told them they were wrongly placed
'Ted's not here is what I witness!'
And then there's superstition
In which a powder did accrue
On the heads of the assassins
Some swore that this is true:
'There's been some crazy goings-on
'In our crowded town beloved
'Some say that if ya walk alone
'By bunyips you'll get mugg'd.'*
*Demons, remember.
Not a single bullet was shot that night
Not a single blade was sunk
The killers all returned the cash
And shambled home within a funk.

AND WHY WAS A SECOND ATTACK NOT POSSIBLE, I HEAR YOU ASK?

Ted was hiding out, y'see
  Him and Uncle Barry
  Just outside of Wagga
  At a pit pronounced 'The Qarry.'
  One of Bazza's daughters
  Whose name is not essential
  Brought them sundry items
  That *can* be classed essential
  Food and water, dunny rolls
  Magazines and tobacco
  Beard wax, apples, gasoline
  (The last was for a shadow show)
  'Cause Ted and Baz were getting bored
  Hiding in the mine
  It weren't much long till Ted said, 'Oi,
  'I reckon that it's time –
  'We grabbed hold of that offer
  'The one in Wangaratta
  ''Cause we're just bloody sittin' here
  'Gettin' dull and gettin' fatter.
  'I think we've gotta take off
  'To a place we'll be respected
  'I tell ya that's not Wagga
  'We're completely unprotected.
  'Tell your dowdy daughter
  'To bring some kangaroos
  'We'll load 'em up and ride 'em out
  'No time for sad hoo-roos.'
  When saddled up and holding reins
  They clucked their tongues real loud
  Then bounced for Wangaratta

Leaving trails of dusty cloud.

WELCOME TO THE WANG, GOOD SIRS

Fred was gonna meet 'em there
    He'd rock up later on
Meantime Ted and Uncle Baz
    Booked a room and used a john
After that they staggered down
    The main and dusty street
Inquisitive of real estate
    And places to eat meat
They found a favoured residence
    And used their ride to do it:
Ted told his kangaroo to hop
    Wherever it did intuit
The roo by name of Benson
    Bounded over to a place
Where two young scruffy locals
    Were watching bull ants race
They said the land they lived upon
    Vacant but for shed
Was left them by their parents
    Both now fully dead
'Might I chance to buy it?'
    Asked Ted with a gentle flourish
As he reach'd for his wallet
    Hoping cash might help to nourish –
These orphans thin who looked at him
    Bewilderment on their faces
Never had they dealt before
    With a man of social graces
A deal was struck and it was good
    (For the orphans more than Ted)
'Cause Ted you might not know it

Had a heart that truly bled –
For those devoid of parents
He was one of them, you see
Both of his had left the earth
By the time he was barely three
Hence why in *The Quotation*
The book eventually compiled
You'll find a many quotable
That sticks up for 'bandoned child
And not just kids but widows, too
They also had his heart
'People should take care of 'em
'And do it like it's art.'
He said there'd be a residence
'On this here piece of land
'But 'fore then Baz both you and me
'Have got some things to understand.'

THE SITUATION

The Wangers who'd made the offer
    Explained things more precisely
The fighting in their town, y'see
Was a conflict ever pricely.
The Wangers were aggrieved by
Three different kinds of 'Zoozites
The Spiel-and-Zucker-buggers
And the Einfelds, who were *half* nice
Ted told them, 'Don't youz worry
''Cause I'll take care o' this
'I'm an expert on Jazoozites
'I've been to many a briss.'
He wandered down and said hello
Checked out their local club
And impressed them with his knowledge
Of their historic family shrub
He could trace their prominent Spokesmen
Way back to that naked bloke
The one with the sneaky missus
Responsible for the yoke –
'That us poor buggers now live beneath
'Since gettin' booted out that garden
'But hey I'm here to tell ya
'I can organise a pardon
''Cause the bloke that you're all waitin' for
'It happens to be me
'I've rocked up here to lead the way
'Straight back to the Big P.
'See the current path you're headin' down
'It's twisted, like you're book
'Whose anecdotes just aren't quite right
'I'll show ya – we can look

''Cause together's how we'll fix the cracks
'That are rippin' through this town
'As one we'll do a reno
'Make a smile out of a frown
'We can start by youz all listening
'To the things I've gotta say
'I'm sure you'll be receptive
'To the good ol' True Blue Way.'
Ted welcomed then a paraphase
Of all that he'd just outlined
And nodded ever happily
That all were now of one mind
'Our book's the lock and you're the key
'And when we stick you in it
'You'll turn so ever nicely
'And Paradise, we'll win it.'
Ted snapped a pair of fingers
(Or a finger and a thumb)
And said with utmost passion
'Good sir you are not dumb
'So what say you *about* it
'Are you with us on our quest
'To prove to all the Mongrels
'That Al alone is best?
'He's even got a theme song
'I'll sing it if you like
'Granted-yes-it's-halfway-done
'But it's enough, you got a mic?'
A stage is what he thought he'd get
But the exit was his gift
There quick arose a mighty *clang*
And Ted was rather miffed
The chunky iron gateway
That locked poor Teddy out
"Biggus Porticullis"

Made him give an outraged shout
But he stroked his beard and thought a bit
And sussed things out some more
Walked round the gated commune
Maybe twice or maybe more
These Jazoozites were quite affluent
Their clothes were freshly pressed
Ted couldn't help but notice
They walked with puffed-up chest
The Wangers all had told him
They did not integrate
They found this quite insulting
'Y'can't say, G'day *mate*.'
A handful of the Christophites
Also lived amid the Wang
Ted paid them all a visit
Smiling gracious as they brang –
A cup of tea, a buttered scone
Listening ears and thoughtful nods
Ted told them how their Bloke Upstairs
Was of the genus *Faulty gods*
'But only 'cause the name ya say
'Isn't quite the right one
'If you'z all just use *Allan*
'You'll have quickly turned the lights on
''Cause that is what I'm here to do
'I'm here to show the truth
'Big Al says I'm a "Warner"
'I should probably build a booth –
'So people can all show up
'And learn the True Blue Way
'I wouldn't have to go to them
'It's a hassle, I can say.
'Not that it isn't worth it
'I'm glad I'm seated here

'All ye goodly Christophites
'Seem full o' fun and cheer.'
Ted hadn't read the guidebook
Their beliefs were based upon
But that issue was "technical"
He'd say why later on
At present all they had to know
Was that Teddy knew the story
Of how Christoph paid the hefty price
So that all could live in glory
For when they'd slang him upwards
On a path toward the sky
He'd flown up like an eagle
Shouting, *This is not goodbye!*
''Cause Chris is gonna come back
'And fight his doppelgänger
'The anti-him, the bloke'll be
'And the war'll be a clanger
'Of course all that,' continued Ted
'Takes place in the Last Days
'All o' this is Judgment stuff
'Hey I like this tea cup's glaze.
'But the bombshell I'm about to drop
'Will *really* blow your brain
''Twas not your friend ol' Christoph
'Who caught the Heavenly Train
'It was in fact a look-a-like
'A bloke dressed up just like him
'Was *he* who got the trebuchet
'Now lives within the lightning
'It might be hard to hear it
'That I understand
'But Big Al's got his reasons
'The bugger's got a plan
'So all o' youz just trust me

'When I tell ya what's the go
'Listen close to Old Mate Teddy
'You'll all be In the Know.'
Ted couldn't understand it
When the Chris'ites all declined
To take in hand the True Blue Way
And have the papers signed
Wasn't it flat-out obvious
That Ted occupied their book?
He was the flamin' central character
Y'could tell with half a look
He kicked a can and walked away
Thinking what he shoulda said
To get his noble message
Through a wall of thickened head
Christophites and 'Zoozites
Were both a cheeky breed
But never mind in time they'd be
All speakin' Big Al's creed.

TRACTION IN THE WANG

Nervous were Waggan Kellyites
    About the conflict in their town
    They close'd shops 'n' grabb'd pets
    'N flooded 'cross the ground
    The wave hit Wangaratta
    The Wangers did accommodate
    Locals opened up their homes
    Terms were coined to celebrate
    Those ahail from Wagga
    Were known as "Refugees"
    While the title of "Aid-worker"
    Was bestowed the Wanganese
    In typical Aussie fashion
    The words were hacked in half
    And 'O's were duly added
    For the sake of having laugh
    The Refos and the Aidos
    Were both a different band
    But all of them were Kellyites,
    One's gottoo understand
    The Aidos signed the dotted line
    Beneath a tall gum tree
    They all were now on Big Al's Team
    Most officially
    Everybody lent their hands
    To have a clubhouse built
    Ted picked up a shovel
    And sank it into silt

The first clubhouse of Wangaratta.

This cutting of a ribbon
Possessed a counterpart
Finally had he penned the song
That would rocket up the chart
The maiden recitation
Of the anthem for Big Al
Was sung by our friend Leroy
A man most musi-cal
He climbed atop the shoulders
Of several former slaves
Each bought by Uncle Barry
To live out the True Blue Ways

He took a breath and yodelled loud
So that all the Wang could hear
A song of rich and dulcet tune
Whose words we'll quote right here

HEHT-HEM

Big Al's the beeeeessssst
   Big Al's the beeeeessssst
   Big Al's the beeeeessssst
   Big Al's the beeeee-eeeee-eessssst
   Ted's his spokeserson (says I)
   Ted's his spokeserson (says I)
   Come on and bob your heads
   Come on and bob your heads
   Come on and wiiiiiii-iiiin
   Come on and wiiiiiii-iiiin
   'Cause Big Al's the beeeeee-eeeeest
   Big Al's the beeeeee-eeeeest
   None is worthy of a head bob except for Allllll
   Copyright Ted Kelly. DCXXIII.

THANK YOU, LEROY.

'Now listen here and listen well
   'I've got some things to speak
   'I'll tell of several *minor* rules
   'Straight and not in Greek.
   'The right hand is one's feeder
   'And it cannot be wipe'd
   'Till clean'd by a roving tongue
   'Be it yours or friends united
   'One should not drink while standing
   'Nor breathe into one's cup
   'Nor lie on back with cross'd feet
   'Nor use right hand to wipeth butt
   "N'when it comes to wiping
   'Don't use animal dung or bone
   'But at least three goodly pebbles
   'Come forth and all be shown.
   'And now we get to clubhouse rules
   'These are all essential
   'Those who do not heed them
   'Are most irreverential.
   'In regard to garlic and onions
   'If one partakes of such
   'Please avoid the clubhouse
   'To prevent a nasal clutch
   '*If* a scent does waft about
   'And one becomes suspicious
   'Then ascertain the culprit;
   'Point a finger most officious
   'Bring halt to all the barracking
   'That the felon be made known
   'But if the crim'nal is a mystery
   'Let the barrackin' keep on goin'.

'If *loudly* someone rips one off
'No one is to laugh
'Those who do are outlawed
'Now let's all learn to bath
'Face then hands to elbows
'Then lightly rub one's head
'Feet and ankles then it goes.
'Should I repeat what I've just said?
'Do this every single time
''Fore steppin' into clubs
'One cannot 'smirch a sacred place
'Ya dirty unclean grubs.
'A second bath should quick be had
'If pee or pÜÜp is plopped
'Even if just wind is broke
'In water get ye dropped
'Remember that the three best things
'A person can ever do
'Is bob the head at the appointed hours
''N treat parents good and true
'Then comes conquerising
'Participate in Big Al's cause
'Do all that and you'll be right
'Your life'll be on course.'

BACKTION TO THE TRACTION

Now that things were under way
    Ted Kelly set up shop
    And began the task of arbiting
    So that arguing might stop
    To him were brought the town's disputes
    That he might make a choice
    He professed a guiding principle:
    To let fairness raise its voice
    He got to hear all kinds of things
    And discriminate the detail
    Of cases greatly interesting
    Like the petty theft of retail
    Usually the quarrels
    Were domestic in their shape
    Like who unleashed the initial punch
    Or 'Ay, that there is rape!'
    One day a few Jazoozites
    Brought forth a pair of people
    Whose actions would be frowned upon
    By the flock beneath a steeple
    Ted naturally inquired
    About the normal protocol
    'We bash em,' was the answer
    ''N smeareth face with charcoal.'
    But Ted replied most pensively
    He thought he could recall
    A certain little verse that made the matter
    Clear for all
    Deep inside the guidebook
    The Jazoozites dearly loved
    It stated with much clarity
    How the fist should be un-gloved

"Pick up your rocks and chuck em
"Aimin' straightly for the head
"Breakers of the wedding vows
"Deserve to end up dead."
The matter was beyond his hands
Ted wiped them straightaway
And said, 'You've gotta do it
"S in your guidebook, 's all I'll say.'
The man was said to Hero Dive
In defence of disgraced diva
She of course went on to cop it
But the gratitude didn't leave her
This all took place in the local square
(Which we'll learn was pretty vast)
It must have been quite shocking
'Cause a witness breathed his last
He hapt to be a member
Of Town Council Wangaratta
He bit the dust and with it rose
Another serious matter
The town was down an alderman
Who could they elect?
It had to be a person
The crowd would not reject
A hand arose and track it down
You'll see that it belongs
To a man whose campaign poster says
He's fond of wearing thongs*
*The Aussie kind. Not the international kind.

THE FIRST ISSUE OF ORDER

Ted Kelly joined the council
    And quick drew up a charter
    It'd make the Wang a simpler place
    'With that issue, one can't barter'

    In legal speak he laid it down
    On a lengthy piece of paper
    In language that to common folk
    Was graspable as vapour
    If the document he had drafted
    Was explained to laymen kind
    Perhaps the flesh that could be found
    Beneath a mountainous rind –
    Might taste quite like the following
    Which tries to make it simple
    (In defiance of all lawyers
    (With their smug and haughty dimple)
    Every single Kellyite
    No matter where they are
    Belongeth to The Family
    And shall not have a bar –
    Of killing other Kellyites

Or sowing seeds of discord
Amid The Family garden
Which is destined to be a-dored
The Family must be aided
If it finds itself attacked
Jazoozites you all hear that
On our side ye must be stacked
And by the way you're not to war
'Less granted Ted's permission
Do this, we'll treat you fairly
Shan't deny a re-venge mission*
*If 'Zoozites should desire one.
Mongrels are excluded
From The Family, yes it's true
And Ted will give the final word
On furore happ to brew
One cannot aid a person
Not regarded as True Blue
I'm sorry there's no Ifs or Buts
Big Al's the boss not you.

Only several months ago
Had Ted moved to the Wang
He was changing laws already
Writing taxes so they brang –
Resources to the Kellyites
Whose endeavours were most worthy
Never mind they treated Mongrels
Like a species hit by scurvy
The disparagement of other groups
Had carried over strongly;
In the Wang just as in Wagga
Other teams were treated wrongly
If an object praised a Bloke not Al
It was grabbed and smashed and chucked
The owner told in blatant terms

'Mongel dawg you go get —·—!'
'Evil gleaming trinkets'
Is what the Team-mates called them
They soaked up Big Al's rightful cheers
Like sponges most absorbent
The assaults were totally justified
On supporters of false order
The Kellyites did it frequently
And their girth was getting broader
One means that individually
But also as a group
The Team-mates feasted on the crops
That made the Wangan soup
Incentives were provided
To be friends with Captain Kelly
The ugly moved with swagger
And stomachs got all swelly
Zoom in close on a growing gut
And regard it metaphorical:
A pithy little sentence
Spoken by an oracle
Things in Wangaratta
Were soon about to pop
It's what happens when a stomach
Has no valve to make a *plop*.

THE WIVES

Before we do a nose-dive
    Into conflict yet to come
    Perhaps let's take a breather
    And have a bit of fun
    Ted got himself some female friends
    Soon after Beryl's exit
    The number is impressive
    He'd tell you, if y'begged it
    The digit shall not be declared
    Explicitly in these pages
    On account of how Ted's followers
    Are famous for their rages
    The first one after Beryl
    Was a lady name of Sheryl
    After her, quite naturally
    Came a chook by name of Meryl

Meryl was quite serious

Good-hearted nonetheless
Known for parsimony
She'd never buy a dress

Luckily she got hand-me-downs
    From all the other wives
    Never did she find herself
    Unable to accessorise.
    Sheryl kept a sparkling house
    There were always toilet rolls
    She was a woman to be relied upon
    And the local champ at lawn bowls
    Farryn, Karen and Sharon
    Were the ones who then appeared
    Farryn means adventurous
    But everything she feared
    She locked herself inside the house
    Surrounded by stray cats
    And quoted oft from memory

The List of Who Begats
Karen was quite docile
Not known for her ambition
T'was her the kids all went to
In the hopes of gained permission
Sharon was the youngest
The youngest quite by far
When she and Ted got married
Head did not touch the bar –
Of the funnest roller-coaster
At the annual town event
Its rides were quite expensive
But to Refos, cash well spent
They married when young Shaz was six
But waited for a time
They did not have relations
Till Shazza was aged nine

Shazza

Despite the gap they got on well
She was actually his favourite
Her sassy wit was pretty sharp
Connoisseurs would often savour it
Maureen, Doreen and Pauline
Were very different girls
Pauline was pretty vulgar
While Doreen loved her pearls
Maureen was noted for her strength
She worked on personal fitness
In this she was a pioneer
Her portraits bear that witness

Maureen

There are two more to speak of
    The first is Geraldine
    Socially quite awkward
    Seldom was she seen

Kylie was the opposite
    Always out not in
    Incorrigibly smiley
    And a finest judge of gin

Kylie

As well as that she loved to chat
      And prance and poke her bottom
      In an upward slant that met the eyes
      Of men who found their names forgotten
      Likely that's the reason
      Ted conjured up the order
      That wrapped his many ladies
      In a most protective border
      He made them all wear doileys
      When visitors came around
      And in public so that gawkers
      Need not trip and meet the ground

If at first they were unhappy
    With this rule, they didn't say it
    "Likely 'cause their mouths are gagged,"
    Said the gossip much convey'd
    Ted built them all a happy home
    Which he called the hacienda
    And there they spent their many days
    Making children of both gender

The one to take most notice of
Is a girl by name of Brittney
On account of how she influenced
Certain elements of history

But let's keep it chronological
That'll help it all make sense
We'll head back now to politics

Watch the rise of great offence

BEFEEL THE TENSION TIGHTENING

Disgruntlement was getting high
 The Wangers all were weary
 Of the Kellyites' tendency
 To say things mean and jeery
 Several well-known citizens
 Brave enough to raise their voices
 Made known their skepticism
 Of Ted Kelly and his choices
 They tried to generate support
 For a mounted opposition
 But most Wangers, apathetic
 Just drank beer and went off fishin'
 She <u>won't</u> be right, said many folk
 Who handed out small pamphlets
 The town of Wang is changing
 Do nothing, we'll be pantless
 Many thought it unavoidable
 That the town would be took over
 And so, to dodge a hassle
 To the Team they all went over
 Ted watched all this with squinted eye
 And never failed to speak
 When someone pressed him for a view
 'Bout the issues of the week
 He made it clear "a dreadful doom"
 Was waiting for the ones
 Who avoided picking up the form
 To see how quill pen runs

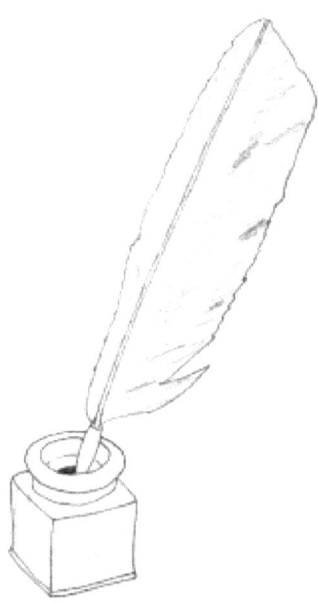

'All ya have to bloomin' do
   'Is sign the dotted line
   'Then there'll be no problems
   'You'll be classed as Me 'n' Mine.'

BOBBIN' FOR THE 'BRU

The practice of the head bob
    Was a useful means of testing
    Which members were devoted
    And who might need some wresting
    If a head did not bob low enough
    Or did not bob at all
    Straightaway there was a culprit
    'Bloody grab 'im by the ball!
    'Get round 'im boys and let 'im know
    'The direction one must face
    'If ya wanna be the target
    'Of Big Al's love and grace.
    'I dunno if I've said it yet,'
    Captain Kell was wont to say
    'The direction we're all bobbing
    'Is aligned with 'Brusalem way
    'Surely *that*'d be a reason
    'For the 'Zoozites to sign up
    'But the bunch o' bloody dropkicks
    'Wanna sip the same ol' cup.
    'I believe if there's no progress
    'Then soon there's gonna be
    'An end to my great patience
    'And invitations to high tea.'

AS ONE MIGHT EXPECT

In time Ted tried to make a deal
    Concerning real estate
    He said, 'Hey there Jazoozite
    'Perhaps y'should vacate.
    'Feel free to sell your land and go
    'But remember that the Earth
    'Belongs to my friend Allan
    'And me, for what it's worth.
    'Of course y'might not realise that;
    'Your hearts are hardened rock
    'And your eyes are sealed by Al, ya know
    'That's why ya cannot grock –
    'That I'm here to bloody warn ya!
    ''Bout the fate you're headed for
    'You're gallopin' for a wallopin'
    'You're bashin' on Hell's door.'

CONJOIN'D TWINS

It wasn't just Jazoozites
    That were giving Teddy trouble
    Some members of the Kelly Gang
    Had faces that went double
    'They're one way on the surface
    'Another underneath
    'That's why I call 'em Twins Conjoined
    'They're two people wrapped in beef.'

ROBBO

'Do you mean beef quite *literally*?'
    Asked Ted's ever faithful clerk
'Or is that just illustrative
'Of a principle at work?
'I might aim for *ambiguous*,'
    Ted Kelly then replied
'I believe a bit o' mystery
'Will keep scholars occupied.
'Have we numbered all our quotables?
'Have we got a sense of order?
'Does the narrative keep one occupied?
''N move along like flowing water?'
'From big to small is how I've placed
'Our magic paragraphs,'
    Said the scribe by name of Robbo
    Holding back a pair of laughs
'The theory is you'll have to wade
'To show oneself devoted
'The shorter rants are at the end
'The front part is quite bloated
'But *I* feel that's a benefit
'It works to our advantage
'We'll suss out who is Truly Blue
'And who is mounting frantage.' *
Robbo meant to say "frontage."
'Excellent,' said Captain Kell
    Rubbing both his hands
'Oh how I long to see this book
'Head out across the lands
'The plans that I've been brewing up
'Are ambitious to say the least
'And all who help to get 'em made

'With me they'll drink and feast
'Here and in the Afterlife
'Where couches are upraise'd
'And there's wine that will not murk the head
'And servants under-age'd.
'But there's work to do, that much is true
'Before we make it there.
'Get your pen and jot this down
'And maybe grab a chair.'

IT BEGINS

Thirteen years after Ferdinand
   Delivered Ted's first quotable
   When Ted was fifty-seven
   And regarded rather votable –
   He spilled the beans from out their can
   His kitty 'scaped its bag
   He even told the gentleman
   Who ran the local rag:

'It's time we started actin' large
'It's time we grew our borders
'It's time that all us Kellyites
'Started drinkin' sweeter waters
'I've appointed several Team-mates
'To roles of leadership
'They'll saddle up their kangaroos
'And take a noble trip
'Some'll be on emus
'Loaded high with many a weapon
'On account of the direction
'The Team'll now be steppin'.
'My newly-minted philosophy
'Several concepts does it juggle
'I spose one of the biggest is
'A word akin with *struggle*
'But a struggle with a *victory*
''Cause we're not here to lose
'Big Al he wouldn't send us out
'Devoid of hats and shoes
'Our Bloke Upstairs has packed a lunch
'So good ya can't believe it
'And if anyone should happ to die
'They'll be the first of all to seize it
'The missions we'll be launching
'Are dangerous, I'll admit
'But those who go upon them
'Will be labelled Hottest...
'I'm lookin' for the perfect word
'To describe the general vibe
'The best one I think *so* far
'Is a term called "conquerise."
'*Conquerising* equates to *winning*
'But *winning's* rather bland
'It needs to sound more oomphie

'It needs to feel heaps grand
'So that's the world I'll go for
'Good ol' *conquerise*
'It's a term for a new era
'Symbolic like "sunrise."'

MISSION # 1

'Remember heading out there,'
    Said Ted Kelly to his troops
    'Allegiance to the True Blue Way
    'Is more important than your boots
    'More important than your family
    'And your country, whatever it be
    'More important than companions
    'No matter their pedigree
    'If anybody back-tracks
    'In the depth of their devotion
    'Their wicked ways'll have 'em set
    'A fiery wheel in motion
    'That Hellish thing'll roll 'em down
    'And squash 'em into pulp
    'Let's please all now envision that
    'I'd better hear a *gulp*.
    'All right then, I am satisfied
    'So mount your megafauna
    'And scream a heady war cry
    'For the mission yaz were born'fa
    'Soon we will cast terror
    'Into every Mongrel heart
    'These wrong-doers living in Evil
    'Shall wake in Hell with frightened start
    'Big Al's Team'll reign supreme
    'It's the only thing we know
    'Keep your chins up, fellas
    'Alright now, off yaz go!'
    Two days' ride beyond the Wang
    On Mission Number Seven
    (The prior six had fallen flat;
    (They were not led by Kevin) –

Kevvy now was at the helm
And waiting to execute
The Captain's writ instructions
Which would tell them who to shoot.
At this point in history
The inland was inflamed
By mechanical innovations
That saw the desert tamed
The continent was gripped by
An industrial revolution
Caterpillar Steam Trains
Were renowned for their toot-tootin'

A chugging cloud most deathly black
Arose into the sky
Kevvy looked beyond his pince nez
And muttered, 'Ooh my my.'
A greedy curl had pursed his lips
He broke into a smile
He waited for the Steam Train

Like a patient crocodile
Rolling heavily across the dirt
Like the tread of a military tank
The powerful locomotive
Equated to a mobile bank

'Alright men, the orders are
'To rob and kill these mungas*
'Those of highest tally
'Shall be gifted packs of bungas*.'
*Munga is slang for mongrel.
*Bunga is slang for cigarette.
'However, let us clarify
'The significance of this day
'I believe the general public
'Might regard it "holiday."
'If that's the case we cannot strike
'It isn't the done thing
'We'll have to wait for week-day
'To it our fight we'll bring!'
A groan of disappointment rang
And someone pointed out
That if they didn't strike today

There'd be no victory shout
''Cause the train'll get to Wagga
'In only several hours
'And then we can't attack it
'We just haven't got the powers.'
Kev saw his men were wilting
So made a quick decision
Called himself a surgeon
And made the first incision
It cut into the sky above
When he raised his gleaming sword
He screamed out, 'Jolly onwards!'
And the men behind him roared

The kangaroos all bounded
The emus ran like devils
The pack of mad marauders

All descended moral levels

They murdered un-armed Aussies
As many as they liked
Then absconded with much booty
Every hostage had to hike –
And was not shy in saying
'It's a public holiday!
'You buggers all are ratbags!

'That's all a bloke can say!'
But they said a great deal more than that
Or perhaps they just repeated:
The Kellyites were *be-yond low*
For the violence they had meted
It seemed that Ted agreed with them
When plunder met his feet
He looked through all the cash and said
'Cripes and holy sheet.
'It was on a public holiday?
'That this was all procured?
'Fellas, that's outrageous
'I thought you'd all matured.'
The carping hostage medley
Ascended in its volume
And grew so irritating
That Teddy gave it no room
'All o' yaz can shut your face!
'I've changed ma bloody mind
'Violatin' a public holiday
'Is a crime of *feeble* kind –
'When compared to what all *youz* do
'Which is block the way to Al
'That's an O-ffence most magnificent
'And for it you'll burn in Hell
'Take this down, young Robbo
'It's a thing I've gotta say
'I want it etched in stone to be
'Inextricable from The Way
'Devotion to paraphenalia
'Is a sin far worse than killing
'So too is turning from the Way
'Your works aren't worth a shilling
'Of all o' those who barrack
'For a team that's not Big Al's

'*A Kellyite is most justified*
'*In removing such Mon-grals.*
'*For can it not be plainly seen*
'*That it's fair in fact and totum*
'*That all of those who spurn the Way*
'*Should be regarded Humans Locum**
* As in temporary.
'*Y'don't deserve to stick around*
'*Al does not want you present*
'*So sign upon the dotted line*
'*Or you'll find things won't be pleasant.*
'Make your choices, hostages
'But remember these boys o' mine
'Will fight until your evil creeds
'Are knocked out your poxy minds
'And by the way, one more thing
'You'll all receive a ransom:
'A number stamped upon your heads
'A sum that shall be handsome
'If your families do not pay it
'I'm sure there'll be a consequence
'An outcome most regrettable
'If sided on the "wrong of fence"
''Cause anyone who joins the Team
'Will straightaway be forgiven
'They'll find that pretty much instantly
'Their chains will all be riven
'So take some time to think it through
'I'm sure you'll see the light
'And make the choice that has ya
'Becoming Kellyite.
'As well as that, I'll say it now
'There's a new law on the continent
'I'll provide an explanation
'I'm sure yaz all are wantin' it

SPOILS OF WAR

'The spoils of conquerising
    'Shall be divvied among my men
    'But not before their 'love'd Cap
    'Receives a small stipend
    'The cash you see before you
    'It forms a precedent
    'The pile shall be divided
    'To me goes twenty percent
    'And that is how it's going to be
    'From this point here on out
    'I get that certain fraction
    'From every rob and rout.
    'Big Al is most forgiving
    'And also merciful
    'That's why his trusted fighters
    'Now find their purses full
    'To commemorate this joyous day
    'Baz will take us out the door
    'He's written a small poem, called
    '*We Lit the Flames of War.*'

THE BATTLE OF GLENDAMBO

The present Mayor of Wagga
    A man named Morris Soak
    Also was a merchant
    Fond of ribald joke

He hired himself a steaming train
To transfer many items
And manned it with an armoured guard
So that villains "get the frightens"

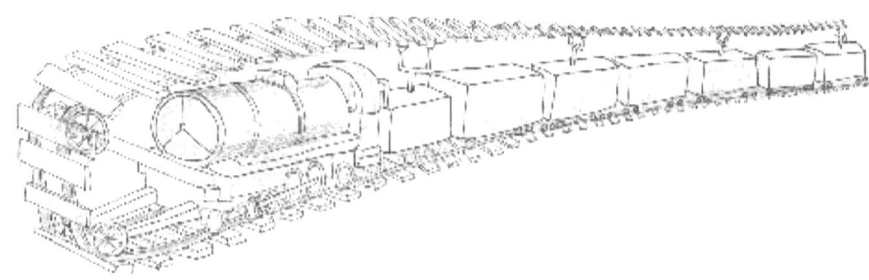

Ted learned of this by way of spies
And said, 'Oh lord, I say
'Let's all go attack it, boys
'May Al give us "the prey"'
His men were mostly vocal keen
But some were quite averse
As Waggans, they had relatives
On that train that did traverse –
A land most unforgiving;
And furthermore they'd heard
The Waggans had been warn'd that
Team interest had been stirred.
By bashing up a pair of slaves
Who were camped and watering wombats
Ted learned the Wags had organised
A thousand men for combat

Some village girls then told some spies
The train was set to land
At a town name of Glendambo
Hid by dunes of sand
The Refos said that they would go
Wherever Teddy wanted them to
The Aidos said something similar:
'Captain, we believe in you
'Hearing and obeying
'We'd plunge into the sea
'And do it to the last man
'We don't fear the enemy
'We are experienced warriors
'In combat most trustworthy
'N look forward to those virgins
'(We like 'em chubby-curvy).'
Ted then received a vision
And told them all about it
'I see the enemy on the ground
'Dead, and do not doubt it.
'And oi can ya believe it
'They've sent their bestest men
'Only to be slaughtered

'By me 'n' all ma friends!
'Alright mates, let's saddle up
'And bounce ourselves away
'We're headin' for Glendambo
'C'mon, I'll lead the way!'
Mayor Morry's expedition
As it rolled across the land
Was attended by the man himself
To provide a guiding hand
He felt a slight suspicion
Or was it more a doubt?
So he bounced ahead the convoy
To consult a trusted scout
'Has anything suspicious
'Hapt to meet your eyes?
'Anything that made ya think
'Ooh, I wonderise?'
'There were in fact two riders
'Standing atop a nearby hill
'Perhaps a close inspection
'Might have your worries killed.'
Mayor Morry went to check it out
He bounced up the mentioned mound
And dropped from off his kangaroo
Spotting something on the ground
It was in fact a dropping
A black and rounded pellet
He picked it up and looked real close
Then decided he should smell it
The next investigation
Would find detail underneath
To ascertain its texture
He bit it 'twixt his teeth
'I taste dates from Wangaratta!
'Of that I'm purely certain!

'Ted's plan has been reveal'd!
'I see past lifted curtain!'
Hopping over to the Waggans
Who'd come out to help the train
Morry told them that Ted Kelly
Had tried to use his brain
'He's headed for Glendambo
'Where he thinks we will arrive
'If we set a new course elsewhere
'He'll get a huge surprise

The leader of the "posse"
   (A term most incorrect)
Was Daddy Ignoramus
A man thought circumspect
Agreeing with ol' Mozza's view
About the enemy plans

A change of course, he did agree
Would leave Teddy wringing hands
'But we're all set to have a fight
'Us blokes who rode from Wagga
'The train can turn, but we'll go on
'I've gotta use the bogger.'*
*Toilet.
'And I hear the Glendam festival
'Is taking place right now
'And I bet there's karaoke
'C'mon, let's win a cow!'
Was Captain Kelly prove'd right
By this strange decision reckless
That Daddy Ignoramus
Followed devils most rebellious
It seems quite out of character
For a man considered wise
To speed toward the distance
With no view beyond the rise
But that is what the D.I. did
He and his merry men
And they struck upon a swampland
When they'd hoped for sunny glen.
Ted was waiting for them
In a valley he had camped in
He and all his Team-mates
Killing time by kicking bean tin
What the posse did not know about
As its many men descended
Was that Kellyites had clogged the wells
Save the one they now defended

So the Waggans now did rally
In a desiccated valley
Un-ideal for launching sally
This would be their grand finale
Ted pointed out their vanity
Their pride was mentioned much
And said that Big Al promised
To destroy them before lunch
For a time there was an impasse
Where no one made a motion
Till a thirsty Waggan stepp'd out
And caused a great commotion
The biggest of the Kellyites
(Hamish, 'member him?)
Trundled out to meet the Wag
With a wide malicious grin
Hamish swung a hefty sword

Its iron blade did hack
The leg off the poor Waggan
Who then copped it in the back.
That Big Al's Team had drawn first blood
Was considered a bad omen
The posse reconsidered plan
Thought their leader just a showman
Regardless of misgivings
They sent a trio representative
To fight three of the Kellyites
In a Prelude Argumentative
Hamish, Freddy, and a random bloke
Were ultimately selected
After the first three representatives
Were summarily rejected*
*Their crust was not upper enough.
In fights of single-combat
Hame and Fred killed their opponents
Then realised that Sir Random
Had been stripped of future moments
Mortally was he skewered
But he hung round long enough
That Ted gave him an answer
That filled him up with chuff
'Yes sir, you are a martyr
'And you're off to Paradise
'So go up and enjoy it, mate
'The drinks've all got ice.
'Big Al has guaranteed me
'If ya strive for his great cause
''N have his lovely creed believed
'He'll open up his doors.'
To all the others gathered round
Ted turned and said aloud
Some things that had some worried

While others puffed up proud
'Everybody slain today
'Advancing not retreating
'Will enter into Paradise
'Big P, and I'm not bleating!'
A Kellyite spat out his dates
And said, 'You mean to say
'The only thing tween me 'n' Al
'Is Mongrels and ma blade?'
He took off running Wag-ward
Sword swinging left and right
Happily dispatched, he was
After half-a-second's fight
Another Kellyite called out
'Oi Ted, what makes Al chuckle?'
The Captain said when soldiers fought
With pure un-glove'd knuckle
The man stripped off his armour
His pants went shortly after
So too did all his underwear
He ignored the gales of laughter
And running for his enemies
With a flapping front appendage
He fought with naked valiance
And quickly met his endage
The call to proper battle
Was when Teddy grabbed a rock
And ditched it at the Waggans
Hoping off would knock a block
He called out, 'Curse your faces!'
And that was deemed the hint
For Kellyites to raise their blades
And commence a raging sprint.
The two opposing armies
Crashed amid a smog

A haze of blade and bullet
And punch and kick and slog
A member of the posse
Had such a thickened helmet
A spear passed through his cranium
Then bent its tip up0on it

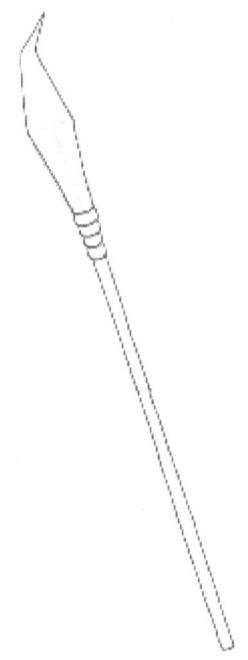

The spear became an heirloom
Passed down by Kellyite
Most often when its owner
Took part in their last fight
Battling for the Waggans
Was a bloke named Uncle Garry
Who'd defended Ted in Wagga
Hence why, 'Gaz you cannot harry.'
The order not to hassle
A relative of Ted's

Annoyed a certain Kellyite
Cutting off familiar heads
'That's flamin' rich,' is what he said
'That Gaz gets outta this
'When here is us all killin' friends
'And relatives we miss.
'I tell yaz all, I'll kill ol' Gaz
'If I see should happ to see him
'Spear him in the guts, I will
'Send him off to a museum.'
Ted heard of what the man had said
And straightaway shouted, 'What!?
'The expresser of that sentiment
'Deserveth to be shot!
'Am I not Big Al's spokesman?
'And is Gazza not me relative ?
'Should the face of my good uncle
'Be disfigured un-decorative?'*
*Ted meant *indecorously*.
Wayne set out to make things right
But must have got distracted
The whinger made it out alive
But henceforth always acted –
Skittish, one would call it
And this went on for years
Ted Kelly and his growing Team
The source of all his fears.
The battle bang'd on so long
Some had to have a breather
And in that resting moment
Someone opened up their wheezer
And said, 'Oi Gaz, your nephew says
'We're not supposed to off ya
'Way to use connections
'Ya nepotistic *pofter*!'

Gaz considered this then answered
'Will ya spare ma friends all, too?'
The reply came back most negative
Garry knew what he had to do
'The women of good Wagga
'Shall not be saying I
'Lived long and fat and healthy
'And left me friends to die!
'Bugger all youz Kellyites
'Come and get me now!'
Someone did they ran up quick
And clocked him on the brow.
As the battle settled down
Prisoners were amassed
The Kellyites did the mustering
And trapped them in like rats
Several members of the Team
Were disgusted by Ted's mercy
'Not-killing all these hostages
'Makes us look like plural turkey!
'To celebrate this victory
'Our first official one
'We should slaughter all these Mongrels
'And watch their black blood run!'
Ted drew upon a quotable
Compassionate in tone
And said that magnanimity
Was the sentiment to be shown.
'But keep your eyes all open
'For Daddy Ignoramus
'If we find him here among the slain
'We'll make his corpse heaps famous.'
Daddy I's philosophy
Go Hard or Just Go Home
Had him swinging sword amid a bush

Chopping heads and cleaving bone
A Kellyite made it close enough
To lop off his left leg
It sail'd through the dusty air
Like cork from tapp'd keg

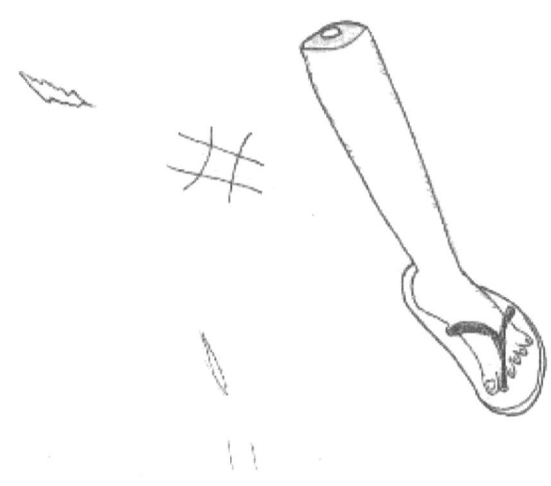

His final words perhaps attest
To a deeply held humility
He was asked a barb'd question
And replied with much civility
The question was, 'How does it feel
'Gettin' shamed by Al?'
He replied, 'How am I different
'From the other blokes you've killed?'
For an answer insufficient
He lost his Mongrel head
Though the Kellyites would have claimed it
No matter what he'd said
They took it back to Teddy
And dropped it at his toes
He clasped his hands and looked above
Then breathed in through his nose

'Here resides the enemy,'
He said after a breath
'The enemy of Big Allan
'Behold his timely death
'Praise belongs to Allan
'Who hasn't got a colleague
'No kid and no protector
'There's no one in the same league.
'He needs no one to save him
'From the clutches of disgrace
'Alright boys, let's get to work
'And clean up this here place.'
Bodies were disposed of
They were chuck'd down a well
Ted peered upon their pile and said
'I know you're all in Hell.'

With them was the father
Of a nearby Kellyite
Who sniffled as his 'loved dad

Took part in downward flight
'I'd hoped him for a member
'Of our most noble Team
'But he would not join our merry band
'For that I want to scream.
'He left the earth a Mongrel
'In fire he now lives
Ted offered consolation with:
'A turd nobody gives.'
To the bodies crammed inside the well
Ted spoke with loft and poise
His Team-mates were confused by this
And asked one of the boys –
To ask their boss a question:
'D'you know these blokes are dead?'
Ted answered with much confidence:
'They understand what I just said.'
Disagreements now the custom
When it came to splitting booty
A wild and roaring fight broke out
And Kev was biffed a beauty.
The Kellyites on the front lines
Said that they were more entitled
Than the Kellyites on the backlines
To Ted they'd simply sidled
With solid hand Ted put an end
To the ranting and the raving
He split the trove in half and said:
'The Team I shall be saving.'
'Every person gets an equal share
'(After I get twenty percent)
'And don't *think* to mourn your loved ones
'To Paradise they were sent.'
Stacking high their wombats
With weapons, cash and load

They set their sights upon the Wang
Back to it they all rode.

THE SPIELBUGGERS

There is an ancient adage
    Which goes somewhat like this:
    Focus hard on just one thing
    There's a lot that you will miss
    Perhaps the poor Spielbuggers
    Were too fixated on their task
    Perhaps they never raised their heads
    To scratch their scalps and ask –
    What's going on around us?
    Are people getting antsy?
    Is the leader of this growing Gang
    Getting aggro mighty fancy?
    Perhaps they should have tuned their sight
    To the goings-on of others
    And made a few extensions
    Toward people who weren't brothers
    Mayhap the band that circled round
    Might not have, quite so tight
    Perhaps the poor Spielbuggers
    Might not'a been put to flight
    The Victory at Glendambo
    Had bolstered Captain Kell
    He returned to Wangaratta
    With many tales to tell
    But found there were some citizens
    Who could not have cared less
    And this, it seems, quite frankly
    Was a source of much duress.
    Ted was quickly spotting
    Grievances all around
    And the source of all this soreness
    Could easily be found.

Those flamin' thick Jazoozites
With their wrapped-up selfish ways
Resisted hard the obvious truth
'Behold my teeth they graze!'
This increased until the pressure
Was enough to crack enamel
Ted found himself so angry
He booted someone's camel
And then set out to look for
A way to solve this matter
He found it in a law-book
Tall as cat and even fatter
'Here it is, I tell you
Said Teddy to the Spiels,
'It describes your misdemeanours
'In prison be your meals
'But ya can't all bloody fit there
'So it's outward you must go
'Grab your things and pack your bags
'This is Captain Kelly's show.'
Forward stepped a 'Zoozite
To focus on fine print
He raised a magnifying glass
And both his eyes did squint
His verdict was that Captain Ted
Had not a valid case
He believed it with such certainty
He said it to his face
Ted frowned at this and then replied,
'Read it once again
'It says it clear and crystal
'A law has been bro-ken
'The treaty all you buggers signed
'When first I came to town
'Has been busted up most grievously

'Hence now you see a frown
'So pack your things and get out
'Quick find yourselves the door
'Or else you will regret it
'Big Al makes me the law.'
This happened in the local square
And today there's some belief
The Jazoozites were objecting
To a particular belief:
That *Big Al had turned Jazoozites*
Into despised and loath'd apes
For doing work on Smoko Day
(A day per week for taking breaks).
'Oh all you Jazoozites
'Be careful what you do
'Remember what the Wags all got
'At the famous Glendam blue?*'
* *'Blue' is slang for fight*
'Don't fool yourself ol' Teddy boy,'
The Jazoozites said in turn
'All of us are real blokes
'Big and strong and stern.'
'Join the Gang, Jazoozites!'
Said the Captain one last time
'Or get the hell from out this town
'It's marked for me 'n' mine.
'Y'know that I'm a Spokesman
'Yet still ya look away
'Only 'cause Al's gracious
'Might ya live throughout the day.'
A raucous fight erupted
The 'Zoozites sprinted off
And locked themselves inside their 'burb
From there they mouth'd off
But Ted besieged their compound

In time they did surrender
With raise'd hands they stepp'd out
Expecting death by render
But T.K was most gracious
He took their wealth and goods
And told them they could keep their clothes
But leave the neighbourhoods
The Einfelds and Zuckerbuggers
Came not to lend a hand
But watched the poor Spielbuggers
Trudge wearily from the land
In time they would regret this
But we'll get to that in not long
Let's stay with Captain Kelly
And watch the Gang do something wrong.

THE BATTLE OF MOUNT DRUITT (WHERE THE KELLYITES GREATLY BLEW IT)

The Aussies back at Wagga
    Were aghast at the Glendam outcome
    So raised some cash, an army too
    And headed out to Give Some.
    Outside of Wangaratta
    The army raised its tents
    And there devised a strategy
    To tackle Ted's defence.
    The Kellyites were hiding
    Behind the Wangan walls
    Which shielded them from arrows
    And well-aimed cannon balls

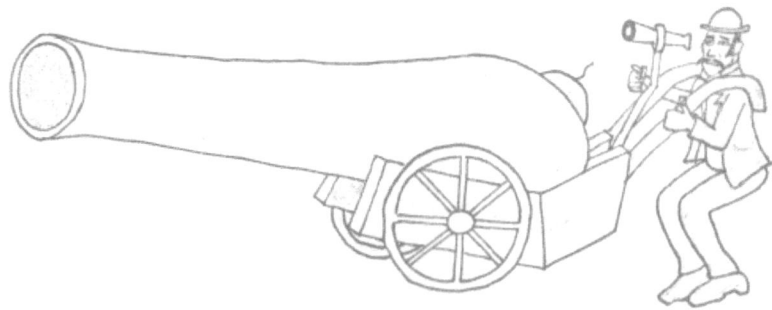

Attendant at a meeting
    Of several Team-mate generals
    Was Ted, who asked them straightly,
    'How should we loose these tendrils?'
    'Let's go out and fight 'em,'

Said one half of the room
The other said to wait it out
'Let 'em keep on goin' *boom*
'Eventually they'll lose their steam
'And tread the homeward track
'And we'll be sittin' comfortable
'No bullets in our back.'
A word that rhymes with *Howard*
Was plinked into the mix
It galvanised the Kellyites
To pick up bats and bricks
Ted slipped into his armour
Putting on an extra layer
And grabbed the sword he'd newly named
Bill the Mongrel Slayer

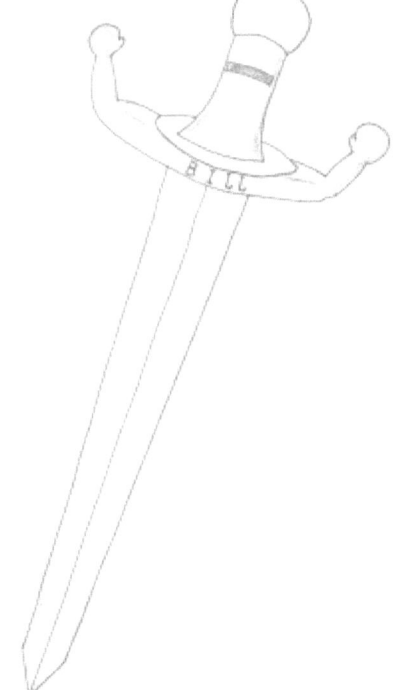

His followers all saw him
Suited up most drastically

And changed their minds about the plan
Saying, 'Perhaps we should just wait and see.'
'Get stuffed ya bunch o' boof 'eds!'
Ted Kelly quick replied
'I'm dressed for war and that's a fact
'Out we all shall ride!
'A Prognosticating Spokesman
'Who has putteth on his gear
'Shall not take it offward
'Till there's battle most severe!'
A thousand nervous Kellyites
Marched out to meet the Waggans
Some thinking they should use their shields
As emergency toboggans
As well as that they turned their roos
From away the fight impending
Three-hundred men went homeward
Saying death they were preventing
Ted Kelly sent them swear words
Then continued for the battle
Saying not to heed their whimpy deeds
'Our courage they shan't rattle.'
At the base of Big Mount Druitt
Where the Waggans were much ample,
Ted saw their roos and wombats
Had dealt the fields a trample
Their furry feet had squashed and trod
The Wangarattan crops
Behold Ted Kelly's bottom lip
Suddenly it drops
And hear him crank an outraged voice
Into its highest gear
And see him lift the blade named *Bill*
To fill the Wags with fear
Angry as all anything

He said he'd give the word
To attack these Waggan mongrels
Have 'em butchered like a herd
Arrow-men and crack-shots
Were made to guard the rear
Fifty in their number
Ted told them not to fear
'Hold your ground no matter what
'Backward do not tread
'To emphasise the gravity
'Of the words that I've just said –
'I'll put on a bit more armour
'And double up my suit
'That I be a scary symbol
'Of how us they cannot shoot
'Their arrows shall not pierce us
'Their cannons are all feeble
'Who will take my sword named *Bill*
'And murder all these people!?'
A hand went up and *Bill* was given
To a man who wrapped a sash
Around his sweaty forehead
Then acted rather rash
He gripped ol' *Bill* and strutted out
To the front of the Kellyite hoardes
Then taunted and paraded
Making fun of Waggan swords
Likely he did not survive
The battle which took place
His sash was coloured red, y'see
He was effortless to trace
And the Waggans were formidable
For a very simple reason
They'd brought along some cheer-leaders:
All the women from their region

Bad form to be a coward
In front of female kind
Testosteranal levels rose
The Waggans all went blind
And rage'd forth into the fight
Their teeth all starkly naked
Driven by a lust for war
Which needed to be slake'd.
The high point for the Kelly Gang
Took place when a Waggan died
And flashed his jolly ball-bag
After copping it in the side
Ted laughed so hard his teeth were showed
His men all fell about
But their happiness was put to bed
When they heard a pain'd shout
A Waggan slave named Tyrone
Who was handy with a spear
Had deal'd with a sheila
Who'd promised more than beer
If Tyrone dropped ol' Hamish
That biggest of Kellyites
Tyrone would get his freedom
And be able to spend his nights –
However he should want to
And that was quite a deal
So Tyrone drew a bead on Hame
And made the big man squeal
Hamish copped a lengthy spear
That went right through his guts
He staggered then fell next to
The corpse with flash'd nuts
Teddy gasped and might have shrieked
(For Hamish was his relative)
He shouted out with gusto

Language most degenerative.
The Fall of Big Bad Hamish
Was a portent filled with gloom
Proved by certain episodes
To which our vision now will zoom
The Kellyites had the upper hand
They were squashing Waggan borders
Till Ted's archers and his crack-shots
Defied their Captain's orders
Inspired by opportunity
They left their held positions
Tempted by the powerful lure
Of generous commissions
The Waggans had been cut off
From their camp, and it was filled
With booty most undoubtedly
'C'mon we won't be killed ' –
Shouted out the archers
And the crack-shots as they ran
Toward a jolly smorgasbord
Flashing riches in a pan

The effect of this was greatly felt
The tide it quickly turned
The backside of the Kelly Gang
Was stabbed and slapped and burned
The more-devoted Kellyites
Stayed behind with thoughts protective
They couldn't let their Captain
Cop a weapon and then not-live
Whenever it did seem that
A Waggan might claim Ted
A Team-mate jumped in front of him
So they'd be hit instead
This behaviour was encouraged
By Big Al's chosen man
Seven faithful Kellyites said
'Teddy, I'm your fan!'
Their bodies lay upon the ground
Ted gave the men a speech

'With me they'll be up in the P.
'Lyin' on the beach.
'And anyone else who joins 'em
'They'll be up there, too
'We'll party like the best of 'em
'And virgins we shall woo!'
A Waggan hapt to grab a rock
And chuck it through the air
It sailed and hit Ted Kelly
On a tooth, and bot lip bare

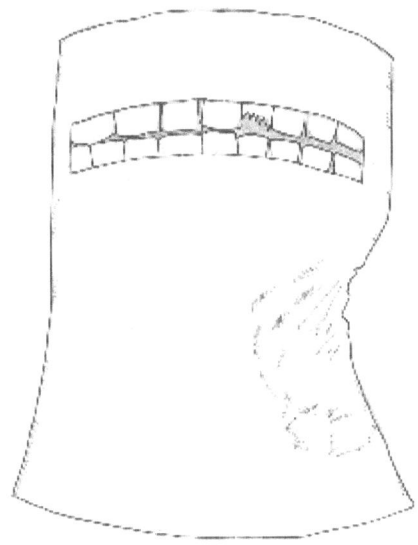

'Bloody hell,' he shouted out
    'That was bloomin' rude
    'Do that in a place more civilised
    'You'll flamin'-well get sued!'
    As consequence of the shooting stone
    Ted's helmet was bash'd in
    His visioned was impair'd
    And so too was his grin

On looking round he saw the Wags
Were closing in real quick
Crafty Captain Kelly
Would need to conjure up a trick
Grabbing hold his kangaroo
He climbed upon its saddle
And fully did intend it
To launch him from this rabble
Instead of that the kangaroo
Sprang but then crashed down
Ted Kelly's doubled armour
Was a far-too-heavy crown

An action roll was then performed

Ted clambered to his feet
And scrambled up a nearby hill
That flight might be complete
From there he watched the battle swing
One way and then another
Countless Aussies squawked and fought
Uncle, cousin, brother.
As per routine the sun did set
The Wags were satisfied
The victims of Glendambo
Had all been equalised
Blood was spilled and fair was fair
They looked upon the gloam
And made the wrong decision:
They chose to head on home
Ted was sent a message
It said that in a year
The Waggans all would come on back
So upwards get your gear
Ted made a solemn note of this
Then put his mind to work
The field of fallen comrades
Was a fact one could not shirk.
Upstairs were pleasure gardens
But down upon the ground
There was a gory battlefield
Throughout it was the sound –
Of people screaming loud in pain
From their wounds, but also 'cause
A bunch of Waggan women
Were cutting off ear and shnozz
Jewellery was their purpose
They'd dry these items out
Then string them all together
A lanyard lobe and snout

The sheila who had sent Tyrone
Fossicked for Big Hame
And cutting out his liver, said,
'I've snuffed ma vengeance flame.
'My burning breast has now been cooled
'I've made up for daddy dear
'Thanks Tyrone, I'm grateful till
'I've lived out my final year.'
The Kellyite cadavers
Were buried 'neath the earth
Ted eulogised on their behalf
And mentioned their new birth
'I testify these merry men
'Wounded by conquerisin'
'Will bleed a florid perfume
'And Big Al'll have 'em risin'
'Every corpse is just a shell
'A carapace of martyr
'Each man they bore the soul of
'Now parties ever harder –
'Than us poor buggers here on earth

'Can ever hope to do
'I say *let's be jealous*
'Big Al says do so too.'
With those words he turned around
And trudged back to the Wang
His bedraggled men behind him
No song was ever sang
Back at home Ted closed the door,
Gave *Bill the Blade* to Britt
Brittney took and cleaned it
Ted sighed and muttered——.
Before the blood had been washed off
Ted already had it sorted
He'd head out in the morning
And have those Mongrels thwarted.

THE NEXT DAY

Teddy and his remnants
  Rode out to catch the Waggans
  But sent ahead before them
  An agent name of Boggins
  Boggins caught up to the camp
  Of Morry and his men
  And Boggins then pretended
  To be the Mayor's good friend
  'Might I now advise you, sir,'
  Boggins said politely
  'That the Kelly Gang is at this time
  'Large and rather spritely
  'Facing them, I do believe
  'Is not the wisest choice
  'Were *I* in that predicament
  'I'd scream till gone was voice.'
  Mayor Morry tapped his smooth'd chin
  And gave a *Hmmm* extensive
  And thanked good Boggins several times
  For the warning most expensive
  The parting word of Boggins
  Said the Kellyites were furious
  And'd sweep to Hell all in their way
  Even bystanders just curious
  The Mayor decided forthwith
  To maintain current course
  That the safety of good Wagga town
  Might keep voice from going hoarse*
  From screaming at the sight of Ted's army.
  Ted and all his Kellyites
  Spent three days camping out
  Perhaps he sent the Bog ahead

To stop a total rout
The speculation there is:
That Teddy got the feeling
If the Waggans turned to face him
The Gang would run off squealing
The chase into the wilderness
It seems was all for show
That Gang morale might elevate
And not be lay'd low
But no one knows the workings
Of the brain beneath the helmet
The curtain veiling Teddy's mind
Stays firm beneath its pelmet.

THE LASHING OF TONGUE

'The reason that all buggered up,'
    Ted shouted long and loud
    'Is 'cause yaz all got greedy
    'And thought just like a crowd.
    'Had ya *not* been pulled by trinkets
    'But stayed and manned your posts
    'We wouldn't now be miserable
    'But absorbin' Big Al's boasts.
    'And to think the best reward of all
    'Dyin' for Big Al
    'Is somethin' yaz missed out on
    'Gosh, it's tragi-cal.
    'Instead we all got nuthin
    'But Big Al, he got somethin'
    'He tested true and found it out:
    'Us, we all are wantin'.'
    Filtering throughout the town
    Was a mist of toxic talk
    That Ted's advice was faulty
    (Someone wrote that out in chalk)
    The murmuring was growing high
    And this could have a consequence
    There might be no attendees
    At the Captain's coming conference.
    Pre-emptively, Ted had to think
    He put his hand to chin
    And asked how might he shift this tide
    And back their hearts all win
    An idea struck a glancing blow
    So strong he rubbed his head
    A soothing touch, he'd have to make
    To soften what he'd said.

Soapbox down, and Teddy up
He spoke most eloquently
Saying, 'Yes we might have suffered
'But the Mongrels are hurtin' plenty
'So never mind, we'll work it out
'The future is our focus
'We'll set our sights ahead of us
''N make Next Time our new locus
'And when You're Done, you are yes done
'And the act of conquerising
'Is the bestest way of all to go
'You'll see the Big P's sun arising
'And the Mongrels they'll all be in Hell
'That's what we've gotta remember
'Us'll all be Upstairs
'Havin' back rubs, every member
'The virgins they will crack our toes
'And tickle every tummy
'And do many other (wink) sorts of things
'Serving food that is very yummy.
'So on the distance set your sights
'It's where we're headin' off to
'And think of what you can learn from this
'There's much, if ya have the mind to
'Here now comes a quotable
'It'll appear in the coming book
'Chapter, verse and sentiment
'For all to have a look.
'It came directly from Upstairs
'Hence why you all should listen
'(Big Al and Ted are very close
'That's our take-home lisson)*
*Ted here pronounced lesson as would a Kiwi, perhaps to make some visitors
feel included.
'To Ted you should always listen

'Cause he knows Big Al's ways
'Automatically do it in days ahead
'He's a Spokesman, is what Al says.
'One last thing, eh Robbo
'Maybe jot this down
'It deserves to be most thought about
'And spread around the town
'It also is a quotable
'Which right now will I speak:
'We do not lengthen Mongrel days
'To make their blessed week
'Rather with the view that
'They'll play up ever more
'Clocking up the reasons why
'Big Al should tan 'em raw
'So stay in your positions
'When Big Al says what is what
'Or else gear up for Hellfire
'It's the message I just got.'

LATE NIGHT VISITORS

There was a certain 'Zoozite
    Zuckerbugger was his clan
    He found himself chagrined by
    The Spielbuggers' outward fan
    And certain Kellyite precepts
    They had him pinching collar
    He said he'd rather die than live
    If Ted Kelly was the fulla –
    Leading things upon the earth;
    It wasn't worth existing
    'Shoot me now Oh Bloke Upstairs
    'You will see I'm not resisting.'
    He must have said these things too loud
    An ear was to the ground
    It swallowed and digested them
    A mouth then made a sound
    It did so with a whisper
    And whispers were returned
    Soon the Zuckerbugger found
    A friend he just had earned.
    One night there came to be a knock
    It rang throughout the house
    The 'Zoozite put his slippers on
    And scared a survey mouse
    'Who is there?' he yell'd out
    To the world beyond the door
    'I'm nought but in me undies
    'Puttin' dacks on is a chore!'*
    *Dacks *are pants.*
    'Hey Frank, it's Steve, remember me
    'I'm sorry it's so late
    'I'm in a hairy 'nundrum

'Need to call a mate.
'I owe a bit o' money
'But I haven't got it on me
'I was wond'rin', Might I borrow it?
'If I leave behind ma gunzies?'*
An affectionate term for firearms.

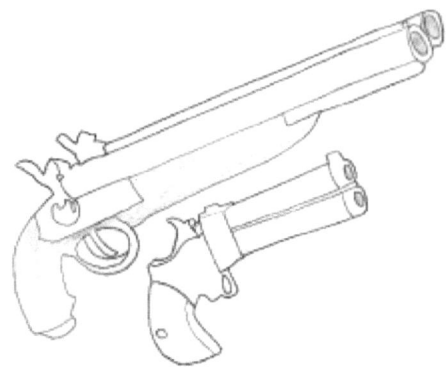

'Tell 'em, Frank,' Frank's wife called out
    'To come back in the mornin'!
    'And tell 'em you're not outta bed
    'Till all the flies are swarmin.'
    'Thank ya luv, but it's alright
    'This bloke I know I can trust
    'He doesn't like Ted Kelly
    'The bond we have can't rust.'
    The Zuckerbugger pulled the pin
    Of the lock upon his door
    Opened up, and looking out
    Saw a group of four or more

'These are all me maties,'
    Said the man whom Frank did trust
    'We've scrounged a good deposit (guns!)
    'Had to wipe off lots o' dust.'
    Frank looked beyond the fly-screen
    His last wall of defence
    And decided he could trust the smiles
    Of these dapper late-night gents
    Opening up and stepping out
    Frank went to shake a hand
    But felt instead a piercing blade
    And failed to understand –
    Why a pool of blood was forming
    On the ground beneath his feet
    Even without moonlight
    It was coloured like a beet

He tried to mumble something
But nothing really came
And then before he knew it
He was marked as fairest game
The Kellyites who did all this
Were propelled by a certain order
An edict which had emanated
From Ted Kelly's family quarter
It was a phrase most simple
It was stated with a glower:
'Kill all the Jazoozites
'Who come under your power.'

EDUCATIONAL REPRESENTATIVES

'Look at this, a letter!'
  Ted said one afternoon
  'Some people wanna learn the Way
  'They've heard that it's a boon.
  'You and you go out there
  'And make 'em all True Blue
  'You've memorised the quotables
  'Yaz all know what to do.'
  Six young and eager Kellyites
  Leapt upon their roos
  And bounded for the Aussies
  Who awaited their good news
  Instead they hapt upon a gang
  That wanted them for ransom
  'Stuffeth that,' was the response
  'I'm dyin' with ma pants on!'
  He died that day, the man who spoke
  And quickly did he do it
  Slowly went his Team-mate
  A bloke last name of Hewett
  Hewie to his many friends
  Was a true and honest character
  Noted for his humour
  An enthusiastic barracker
  He was taken off to Wagga
  Sold quickly as a slave
  His owner mustn'a liked him
  Poor Hewie got trebucheted
  Off he flew, into the sky
  A Christoph imitator
  His mortal form regarded with
  The value of a 'tater.*

*As in potato.
But that was the just the culture
The way that things were done
Etiquette was kept intact
By quickest blade and gun

JUST QUICKLY...

Ted Kelly knew this very well
    It's why he duly sent
    Another batch of educators
    To straighten something bent
    There was a certain Mongrel
    Who wanted Ted's position
    He was building up his own gang
    Ted heard and planned a mission.
    To his rival's jolly camp
    He sent a jolly mole
    Who got in jolly close one night
    And scored a jolly goal
    A package was delivered
    Straight to the hacienda
    Ted opened it and found the head
    Of his rival, 'Oh the splendour!'
    With gratitude he gave a gift
    To the high-achieving mole
    It was in fact Ted's walking stick
    A slim and gnarly pole!

And more than that: a voucher
    For the mole to make the P.
    'Ya will not have to burrow,'
    Said Ted, so wittily.

ALRIGHT, BACK TO IT...

Looking down and seeing
   A letter on his desk
   Ted disembowelled it, thinking,
   'Tis surely bill grotesque.
   Instead it was an invite
   To come and teach the Way
   'Stuff that, mate,' said Captain Kell
   'I've learned, is all I'll say.'
   But *Umming* chased some *Ahhhing*
   And soon he changed his thoughts
   And outward went a teaching pack
   Seventy men, all wearing shorts
   All but two were slaughtered
   And the one that did survive
   Shortly had his mullet cut
   A crime one can't abide
   And so he pledged to 'venge himself
   This Kellyite without mullet
   The desire was so powerful
   It was crawling up his gullet
   Thanks to technicalities
   Familial in their form
   He was setteth free and setteth'd off
   To climates far more warm
   On the way he fell into bounce
   With a pair of Aussie men
   Whom he quickly realised
   Were of the tribe that killed his friends.
   He formed a plan and got it done
   Indeed that very day
   He killed them as they had a kip*
   Then bounced himself away

A short sleep.
Back in Wangaratta
He told of his adventures
Ted would have spat out all his teeth
Were he a man of dentures
'Cripes and bloody hell ya fool!
'With that tribe I had an alliance
'Now I owe 'em haemo cash
'And I'm short on dough suppliance.
'Y'know what this'll flamin' mean
'I'll have to get a loan
'And the bloody Zuckerbuggers...'
Ted sighed and gave a groan.

THE BLOODY ZUCKERBUGGERS

Ted borrowed a hat (to take it off)
    And paid the Zucks a visit
    His query was slow in coming
    Some humility was mixed within it
    The Zuckerbugger lenders
    Leaned back in their camel-hide chairs
    And fixed the Captain fixedly
    With seven pairs of stares
    'The Zuckerbugger Bros. Inc,'
    Said the brother on the left
    'Needs a little more convincing
    'That we're not the marks of theft.'
    The brother on the right spoke up
    And then the middle three
    The second from the left spoke up
    They all seemed to agree
    What they all agreed upon
    Depends on who you question
    Ted Kelly said they hatched a plan
    Akin to insurrection
    He hurried back and closed the door
    Of the Clubhouse Wangaratta
    Looked round out at all his followers
    Saying, 'Sirs there is a matter –
    'That we all need to speak about
    'For I am of the view
    'That something natured dastardly
    'Has been attempted by Jazoo.
    'They bloomin' tried to drop a rock
    'On-to ma bloomin' head

'It missed me by a fraction
'Bloody hell, I could be dead!'

The Kellyites were outraged
They sprang onto their feet
Shouting out and clenching teeth
So hard they could grind wheat
'Let's bloomin' go and get 'em!'
Was the suggestion of young Wayne
'We'll teach 'em not to run amok
'We'll cause 'em lots o' pain!'
Knives and bats and bricks and guns
Were gathered quick and smart
The Team-mates poured out on the streets
And *hurried* quick and smart.
The Zuckerbugger residences
Were part of a community gated
This fact along with others
On the Kellyites greatly grated

Ted leaned in ever closely
To a metallic kind of spout
A tube that turned into a horn
From which his voice did shout
'Oi you there, Jazoozites
'You bloody Zuckerbuggers
'Come out here and give your ear
'You dirty mother-pluggers
'I've got some things to tell you
'Some charges to be laid
'And if you're not inclined to
'Your gates'll all be flayed!'
Another horn much higher up
Abruptly came to life
From out of it there was a voice
Saying, 'Not upon your life.
'State your business, Kelly;
'The things you're bangin' 'bout.
'We're interrupting nap time
'To hear you rant and shout.'
Ted drew a breath and let it out
In a stream most hard and torrid
A series of accusations
And language highly florid
'Ya bloomin' tried to drop a rock
'On-to ma bloomin' head
'It missed me by a fraction
'Bloody hell, I could be dead!'
Perhaps in fear of lawsuit
The 'Zoozites all denied it
But Ted Kelly was most adamant
And with him his Team-mates sided
'We saw him there upon your roof
'A killer vile and heinous
'If we find the man particular

'We'll rip him a new manus!'*
*Scholars are uncertain about the meaning of the word manus.
'So open up ya Mongrels
'And let us come and bash ya
'We've got yaz all surrounded
'Tell your flowers We're gon' mash ya!'
Having hemmed the Zuckerbuggers
They crashed against their compound
The walls were those of mighty fort
But soon they would be knocked down
The Team-mates all bent downwards
To lift up battering ram
Ted called out for some matches
And laughed at every BAM!
He gave a rousing speech that day
Which articulated precisely
That Big Al deals with 'Zoozites
Oh so ever nicely
'The aim of the common 'Zoozite
'Is to assist in earthly mischief
'But every flame they kindle for war
'Big Al will surely sniff it.' *
*Ted meant snuff it.
And with that illustration
Ted struck himself a flame
And placed it to a tawny leaf
Of a tree that went KA-BLAME!
Date trees left and right went up
Like rockets in the sky
They must have been combustible
'Jeez those things can fly!'
From out the earth their roots all tore
The Kellyites crouched and cowered
Unleashing ample swear words
Each feeling much empowered

The Zuckerbuggers watched their chattels
Sailing across the sky
And decided it was probably time
To kiss the Wang goodbye
But a sudden hope of recourse
Sparked within a head
'Quickly, call the Einfelds!
'We've a contract signed in red.'
On account of 'Zoozite affluence
They possessed a telegraph line
It travelled out across the town
A suspended licorice vine
Sitting down and pedalling hard
They tapped a hasty script
'Come out here and help us, please
'Before our shirts gets ripped.'
The message made its way along
The elevated cable
And found the Einfelds sitting down
Breakfasting at table
The juice was poured, croissants were baked
The flowers were all fluffed
'Tell them maybe later,
'When our stomachs are not puffed.'
'The Einfelds are not coming
'They're too busy, they have said
'They've left us on our own, it seems
'To deal with Captain Ted.'
The fact that was most obvious
Related to escape
There seemed to be no way of it
Mouths were all agape
'What the *bleep* are we to do
'We cannot fend them off
'The Kellyites are closing in

'Like hogs toward a trough.'
'I say that we should strike a deal,'
Said an elder of the group
'Make it out with skins intact
'Our losses we'll recoup.
'Give 'em bloody everything
'That's all I have to say
'But leave some room for haggling
''Cause that's the 'Zoozite way.'
They bartered an agreement
Captain Kelly set the terms
The Zuckerbuggers must leave the town
And back they could not turns
The haggling was successful
For the 'Zoozites all could keep
Whatever they could carry
This included several sheep
They loaded it most quickly
On the backs of giant wombats
Even pulled apart their houses
Right down to insulation bats
Wood was at a premium
At this here time and juncture
Hence the 'Zoozites kept it
To avoid financial puncture
The only thing they couldn't take
Were elements of armour
Aside from that, they took it all
Mother, child and farmer.
Escorted thence from out the town
There was a lengthy line
Of disheartened Zuckerbuggers
Their faces streamed with brine
Ted Kelly watched them heading out
And heard somebody say

They were off to Arayonga
To start a brand new day
After that he clapped his hands
And rubbed them both together
Then turned to all his Kellyites
And made mention of the treasure.

OF THAT TREASURE...

'Because there was no fighting
 'All we did was bang some walls
 'There are in fact no fighters
 'To divvy up the spoils
 'All of this, it goes to me
 'And now to other matters
 'I feel it deep within my breast
 'That gossip pitter-patters

OF THE CRITICS...

'If yaz all are wondering
    'About all this "destruction"
    'And how previously I have frowned upon
    'Such wanton deconstruction
    'Please allow me to inform you
    'And this is straight from Allan
    '*He* made all those 'Zoozites
    'Drink his vengeance by the gallon
    ''Twas Al who had them tearing down
    'Their sheds and all their houses
    'And the burning of their date trees?
    ''Twas natural, like beating spouses.
    'The Zuckerbuggers should have listened hard
    'And joined the True Blue Age
    'Instead both them and us right here
    'Will turn a whole new page.
    'Thank you.'

TED'S ADVICE ON WOMEN

Backwards several paragraphs
    Mentioned ever quickly
    Was a reference to domestic battery
    Which we'll stir a bit more thickly
    Of women, Ted had many views;
    His household was a welter
    From which there flowed some quotables
    'That'll teach ya how to belt 'er
    'A woman's like a rib, good mate
    'Y'cannot straighten 'er out
    ''N if applying too much pressure
    'You'll hear a *snap* ring out.
    'I've seen the fires down in Hell
    'And I have gotta tell ya
    'The residents are sheila folk
    'Ungrateful things, we've fell fer
    'Never have I come across
    'A deeper dearth of intelligence
    'Or ignorance about the Team
    '(But yes we like their elegance)
    'A careful and intelligent man
    'C'be misled by many a lady
    'Their natures, it is obvious
    'Are coloured somewhat shady
    'Hence why y'can only trust 'em
    'To the sum of fifty percent
    'A woman's word is half a man's
    'That is from Big Al sent
    'A lack of fondness for the Team
    'Explains the reason why
    'They cannot barrack when On the Rag
    'For that we all should cry.

'So there y'go, remember this
'It's with a humble stick
'A bloke can beat his missus
'But lightly, that's the trick.
'And remember girls, throughout the night
'The angels'll curse your sleep
'If y'keep your husband from your patch
'And stop him ploughin' deep.
'Kind you are for all your life
'To the women in your life
'But if they spot a single fault
'Jeez there will be strife.
'To get hold of the benefit
'Y'gotta do what I said:
'Accept her as that curvy rib
'Crooked in the head.'

THE WAGGANS

Perhaps your good self can recall
    An oath made by the Waggans
    To come back in a year or so
    And administer some floggins.
    The time had come, they armied up
    And mobilised on out
    Arm'd to the brows, they were
    But they ran into a drought
    Mayor Morry, he was leading
    This military expedition
    The matter fell upon him
    He made a hard decision.
    'Alright men, let's turn around
    'This land is getting dry
    'Chewing-grass is what we need
    'For fauna milk to fly
    '*Thirst* is not a pleasant thing
    'And it I would like to avoid
    'So let's return to Wagga and
    'In a year be re-deployed
    'A year again, from this day now
    'Is when we'll make our strike
    'And if we do it properly
    'Upstairs will Teddy hike.'
    They waited for the year to pass
    Then saddled up again
    Arm'd to the brows once more
    Were all these Waggan men
    Many spies throughout the land
    Were working for the Captain
    Ted heard the Wags were coming;
    Saw the problem he was wrapped in

The Kellyites had gone to seed
For ages they'd not fought
Their only fight was a non-event
When neither side stepped forth.
Heads were put together
They *doonk'd* in the doing
A cunning plan was quickly hatched
So good they all were cooing
If they dug a trench to stop the Wags
From getting to the Wang,
Wags wouldn't get a chance to use
All the weapons that they brang
Shovels quick were handed out
They began the excavation:
A trench of great proportions
Deep and wide as a small nation

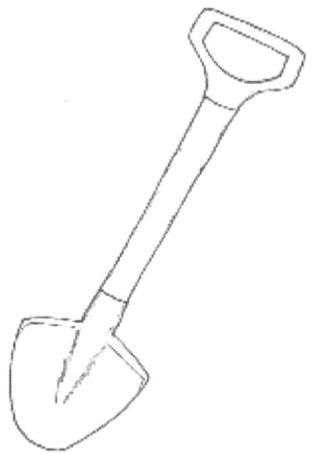

Eight days it took, to finish it
There was grumbling all throughout
Ted mouth'd off a quotable
To stanch its oozing spout.
And then there came some sudden news
Which threatened to exhume it
The grumbling could be tapped anew
The Gang could be consume'd.

THE NEWS

In Wagga was a 'Zooite
> The Einfelds were his friends
> He went to Wangaratta
> To achieve some certain ends
> Knocking on the iron gate
> With *Einfeld* written solid
> He finally gained an entrance
> To a garden far from squalid
> A certain man of influence
> Who called himself Big Francis
> Disperse'd very quickly
> The usual song and dances
> 'Tell me what you're here for
> 'So I can tend my roses
> 'It's how I like to spend my time
> 'That's just the way it goeses.'
> The Waggan's words all tumbled out
> At first they were rejected
> But gradually Big Francis thought
> Perhaps they're not confected
> The Waggan 'Zoo who'd hit the Wang
> Had taken off his hat
> And with a lot of earnestness
> He'd told Big Francis that:
> 'Behind me is an army
> 'And in front of all o' you
> 'Is a golden opportunity
> 'To squash the ol' True Blue
> 'Hell bent on crushing Ted, we are
> 'And not leaving till we've done it
> 'And youz can be a part of it
> 'This war, help us run it.

'We've done a deal with others, too
'*They're* all helpin' out
'We're gonna hit ol' Teddy boy
'And knock the beggar out.
'Surely y'can see that
'The buggers Spiel and Zuck
'Make clear the perfect reason
'With us it's smart to truck
'What say it, eh, Big Francis
'Will the Einfelds lend a hand
'And scatter all these Kellyites
'Far and wide across the land?'

THE DECISION AND WHAT FOLLOWS

Before the sun had even set
    Ted knew of BF's choice
    His spies were overhearing
    Every Einfeld voice

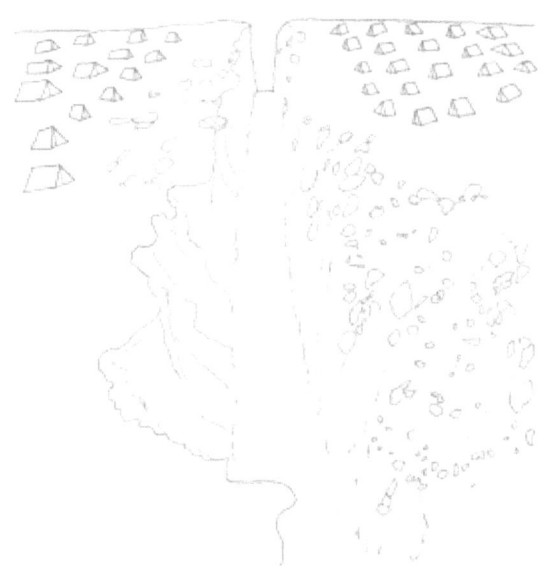

Thick on the horizon
    Were many Waggan tents
    Camped right upon the very edge
    Of the Kellyites' trench.
    The Team was rather worried
    But their Captain was excited
    The Gang was gonna see this through
    The Waggans'd be blighted

Mayor Morry was encountering
A blight of sorts already
The hat of who was general
Was anything but steady
The Wag of course was filled with clans
And each demanded a say:
To clog the appetites of pride
There was a general for each day

This custom of rotating
    Proved very irritating
    Every bloomin' sunrise
    Had the band re-orchestrating
    'Bloody hell,' Mayor Morry said
    'This pains my bottom truly

'The system is a dumb one
'Makes our army all unruly.'
But on they went regardless
Each general making plans
And giving lots of orders
That all vanished in the sands
Ted heard all this and laughed a lot
And used it as a mode
Of cheering up his followers
Who complained about the load
'Don't worry boys,' the Captain said
'I know how yaz all feel
'Get shot at even on the bog
'Cripes, what's the deal?
'Time is dragging on, I know
'Yaz all are gettin' edgy
'But keep your chins all skyward
'And pick out every wedgie
''Cause we're all gettin' off our bums
'Our rumps'll all be used
'We're writin' out the history
'Of How the Waggans Losed.
'As well as them the Einfelds
'Are gonna cop it salty
''Cause all those silly buggers
'Made a choice you'd label faulty
'They're thinkin' that the Waggans
'Are gonna form a link
'With a bunch of other Aussies
'But man they're gonna blink –
'And then they're gonna miss it
''Cause I've conjured up a plan
'To the last 'Zoozite community
'I have sent an agent man.
'You know what he'll be saying?

'Once stepping through their gate
'Einfelds, how ya goin'?
'It's me your good old mate!
'And then he's gonna ask them
'Of the Waggans, have ya heard?
'Their campaign isn't doing well
'It's a barely-floatin' turd.
'And oi, I heard it somewhere
'That youz've got a bond
'That youz and all the Waggans
'Are friendly mighty fond
'That's why I thought I'd come here
'And serve it to you straightly:
'Maybe suss it out a bit
'Before committing greatly
''Cause the Wags are all outside o' town
'And if they don't get in
'If they pack pack their bags and hit the road
'Think o' who gets left within
'It's not the blerry Waggans
'(They'll head home upon their feet)
'It's the Wangarattan citizens
'The Einfelds, aren't they sweet.
'But I might be able to help you
'An idea has hit me hard
'What if all you Einfelds
'Played the cute 'n' crafty card?
'Before yaz fight the Kellyites
'Maybe get the Wags to prove
'They're of an order genuine
'Tell 'em, Give a bit o' proof.'
Ted halted in his story
'Cause someone raised a hand
Asking, 'Can ya say it clearer
'So all-us understand?'

'Sure I can,' the Captain said
'Listen to me close.
'Quickly shall I speak it out
'A description un-verbose:
'The Einfelds and the Waggans
'Together will attack
'But I have tricked the Einfelds
'That their plan might be set back
'They're asking for the Waggans
'To prove they won't just run:
'If you are for this conflict
'Giveth up your son
'Or better make it plural
'A few will tie things nicely
'They can help us over this side
'They'd be soldiers ever pricely.'
Ted paused again, but this time
He was stifling a giggle
'Yaz won't believe what I have done
'It'll have 'em higgle-piggle.
'Hear it now, I've said it prior
'War, it is deceit
'And to the mongrel Waggans
'I sent sower with a seed
'To Moz he had a quiet word
'(This man who is an agent)
'Mayor Morry, as he's comm'ly known
''Parrently finds himself complacent
'Or is the word *complicit*?
'Yeah that's what I'm lookin' for
'Complicit is the Mayor named Moz
'In the plan that'll drop his jaw
'This is what the agent said
'(And he spoke it all real smooth-like
'(I told him "Be heaps oily

'("A *snake* is what to move like"):
'*The Einfelds, Moz, they're sneaky, mate*
'*They're aimin'to cross ya double*
'*They're cookin' up a cheeky plan*
'*To give you Waggans trouble.*
'*What they're gonna do is,*
'*They'll ask for some-ya sons*
'*And when they do, ya'll know it*
'*The buggers are not chums.*
'*'Cause what they're gonna do is,*
'*Hand 'em over to Ted Kelly*
'*And then he'll have some hostages*
'*Ya might even lose a rellie!*
'*Imagine if he sent one*
'*Flyin' over trench*
'*Trebucheted right through the air*
'*To land on your general's bench.*'
'That last bit about the generals
'Is me just havin' fun
'Pokin' at the silliness
'Of the way their army's run
'And the moral of my recount is:
'We have but nought to fear
'The Einfelds will not dare to move
'Against our naked rear
'And *how* is it I know this?
'Behold the flashing *that* way
'That is a called a heliograph
'And a message doth it convey:
'*The "Zoozites asked for Waggan sons*
'*Now Trust is all uprooted.*
'*The alliance is in tatters*
'*Their plans have all been booted.*
'Three cheers for Al is what I say
'Now all we do is wait

'And duck the fluggin' cannonballs
'Whose sound I fluggin' hate!

THE OUTCOME

The Battle of the Trench
    As it's now historically known
    Concluded after twenty days
    With a drawn-out Waggan groan
    The weather was most miserable
    Supplies were getting low
    Mayor Morry had a gutful
    And said, 'Stuff it, I'm gonna go!'
    He saddled up his kangaroo
    And bounced the thing on out
    A bewildered Waggan infantry
    Didn't strain to hear him shout:
    'Stuff all this, is what I say
    'The camels and wombats are croakin'!
    'If youz call this a permanent camp
    'My friends, you are all jokin'!'
    The Waggans watched their leader
    Bounding toward the sunrise
    Scratched their heads for a period
    Then attempted all to summarise –
    Their current situation
    Which really wasn't good
    'Should we stay and keep on fighting?'
    'Nah, don't think we should.'
    Taking down their tents
    And packing up munitions
    They weighted down the wombats
    'N abandoned their ambitions
    Captain Kelly was the victor
    At the Battle of the Trench
    'Twas he who came out smiling
    Not the generals on the bench

And how would Teddy celebrate?
He already some clues
The party that he had in mind
Would be attended by Jazoos.
Ferdy did confirm it
When dropping out the sky
'Hang on a moment, Captain
'Some fur still needs to fly.
'Go and have yourself a bath
'But then get straight right to it
'Those dirty rotten Einfelds
'My my, they surely blew it.'

THE EINFELDS' OUTCOME

After Ted had had a bath
    He cleaned ol' *Bill the Blade*
    Armoured up, stepped out of house
    For the Einfelds he then made
    Behind him were his faithful men
    Their eyes like burning coals
    An observer can only cringe at
    The nature of their goals
    'Hey you there Jazoozites!
    'You brethren of apes!
    'It's I, Captain Kelly!
    'Big Al brings you disgrace!
    'As well as that there's vengeance!
    'So come out here and get it!
    'Every single man and child!
    'And your women, or you'll regret it!'
    A siege played out for many days
    Twenty-five to be exact
    Einfelds versus Kellyites
    And the Einfelds slowly cracked
    Never had they taken
    The Captain and his boys
    To be a serious threat to them
    'They're just morons makin' noise.'
    They'd smirked when Ted had claimed to be
    The main character of their book;
    And that everything inside it
    Was designed to make one look –
    And see that Al was planning
    A specific culmination
    A Day when Captain Kelly
    Would lend a hand to every nation

For Ted Kelly was the main event
In the history of human kind
On the coming Day of Judgment
He would unloose the people's bind
No one else could do it
Not him or him or him
And definitely not ol' Christoph
That bloke is not Al's kin
''Cause Big Al does not have a child
'And the fellas in your book
'They are not nearly capable
'Of serving Al a look
'I am he, Jazoozites
'The one who'll intercede
'The one who'll stick up for yaz
'The one you're gonna need
'For on the Day of Judgment
'I'll be laden with a task
'Given me by Biggest Al
'In his glory you can bask
'You know what he has said to me?
'Know what he's gonna say?
'When he and I are chatting
'On biggest Judgment Day?
'Raise your head young Captain
'And speak 'cause you'll be heard
'Your intercession'll be accepted
'Your requests won't be deferred
'I'll give you, sir, a limit
'On who you can approve
'To escape the fiery flames of Hell
'And to the Big P move.
'No one else can do it
'Not him or him or him
'The Jazoozites and the Christophites

'*Their books are far too dim*
'*They do not say it outright*
'*Subtextual is the stab*
'*Ted Kelly is the only bloke*
'*Who can aid your Heaven grab.*'
The Einfelds asked a friend of theirs
Who somehow paid a visit
What might happen if they raised their hands
And braved the outside blizzard
The view of their good visitor
Was that Ted would cut their throats
He said this with a finger
No words for future quotes
The Einfelds were most hungry
For they had not stocked their larders
And they had no washing powder
Sullied were their garters
Never in their memory
Had they been without resource
Their money-focused values
Made the clan a working horse
The cash at their disposal
Had no beach on which to lap
It was trapped inside their compound
This dealt the 'Zoos a slap
Never had they found themselves
Without the strength of purse
If you want it, then you buy it
Feeling sick, then rent a nurse
The gardens in their compound
Were what they'd always tended,
Heedless of the plants outside
Whose growers were offended
It wasn't just the verdancy
Which had outsiders miffed

But a mark'd lack of interest
That made one feel slightly biffed
Too late now to set things right
The Einfelds faced a choice
Stay inside and starve to death
Or go outside and use one's voice
Surely an agreement
Could be hashed-out well and good
Truly they could strike a deal
And bring peace to the neighbourhood
Big Francis and associates
Stepped past the Einfeld gate
Hands raise'd high within the air
Cautious was their gait
Captain Ted, high on roo
Watched them all approach
Bill the Blade was at his side
To achieve a body broach
But only if these 'Zoozites
Fail'd to submit
The True Blue Way was calling them
'Gentlemen, please all sit –
'And tell me why you've come here
'To speak to me today
'Am I right when I believe that
'You're desirous of The Way?'
Francis was the man who spoke
And he did it most efficiently
'Ted,' he said, 'we cannot join
'It would grieve our kind proficiently.
'The Way is not for us, y'see
'But it is of course for you
'So what might be the deal we strike
'That *we* all stay 'Jazoo?'
Ted clucked his tongue and thought a bit

And said, 'Oh me oh my
'The outcome of this present trial
'Cannot be chose by I
'Fellas, where is Sammo?
'Still laid out on a stretcher?
'Seek him out and bring him here
'Send your fastest fetcher!'
Annoyingly for all involved
They sent the fastest chap
But paired him with a portly bloke
Who move'd without zap
Finally they brought him forth
Sammo on a bed
Shotteth'd in the arm, he was
Tomorrow he'd be dead
His wound was suppurating
The infection, it had spread
The verdict of modern scholars is:
He was not right in head
But Teddy put it to him
'Whatta ya reckon, Sam?
'Give us all the answer
'That'll get us out this jam.'
Sammo heard the details
Then forced his tongue to move
Teddy said Big Al and kings
Greatly would approve.
The verdict was a simple one
Uncomplicated as could be
Sammo, in fact, was proud of it
'Twas his final legacy
'Cut off all the blokes' heads
'Make slaves of chicks and kids
'To the Team will go those latter kinds
'Kellyites, make your bids!'

'Alright, let's get started
'We haven't got all day
'For my name is Ted Kelly
'And youz do what I say!'
The Kellyites all rounded up
The Einfeld blokes with hair*
And took them to the marketplace
The Wangarattan square
*Of the pubic variety.
There they got to business
They dug a massive pit
An entire day, it took them
To mark and diggeth it
Wiping hands and dusting legs
They broke out swords and knives
And set upon the 'Zoozites
For several days and nights
Eight days, in fact, it took them
To cut off all their heads
Many were surprised at
'All those shades of reds.'
Eight-hundred was the number
Of blokes who lost their skulls
Dump'd in a mass grave
They were picked at by the gulls.
Ted and his wife Shazza
(Who was eleven at this time)
Watched the scene most avidly
Sipping tea to cope with clime.

The only woman killed that day
    Had been chatting with young Sharon
    Till she stood and slowly walked away
    Like her soul was all but barren
    Happily she knelt upon
    The ground beside the ditch
    And asked a helpful Kellyite
    To scratch her final itch
    He took a sword and held it close
    She smiled and closed her eyes
    He cut her Mongrel head off
    Gave her body to the flies
    Another bloke who did the same
    Was ancient as could be
    And opted not to live on earth
    If devoid of all his family.
    When dirt was sprinkled on the grave
    And earth was patted down

They commenced the distribution
Of some women of the town
The females of the Einfeld clan
Were sorted into categories
Then Teddy paid a visit
To analyse the pedigrees
He chose the most attractive
And kept her for himself
And asked for all the ugly ones
To be taken off the shelf
'Or rather sell 'em onwards
'Y'could make a bit o' money
'Granted they're not happy now
'But in time they might be sunny.'
The property of the Einfelds
Formed a giant pile
Ted was due his twenty percent
His men, they all did smile
Kellyites each made away
With a barrel full of treasure
'But hang on boys, there's one last thing
'A precautionary measure.
'The town it must be safety-proofed
'We must kill all the dogs
'Ferdy paid a visit, saying
'*Those things are rotten bogs.*
'If a dog is in a person's house
'An angel won't come near
'So go out there and kill 'em boys
'Then there's nought to fear!'
The Dogocaust that followed
Was brutal, quick and bloody
There was a lone survivor
A canine brave and ruddy
Boris was the pooch's name

And he was saved because
He guarded Wangarattan fields
Good ol' "Lucky Boz."

A LITTLE BIT MORE VIOLENCE
PART I

Two faithful Kellyites left the Wang
    To visit ol' Mayor Morry
    Their orders were to take some blades
    And plug a source of worry
    They hadn't been in Wagga
    For a good long span of time
    So walking through its outer gates
    They thought, *Gosh, what a crime –*
    It'd be to bloomin' leave here
    Without visiting the Pub
    We could barrack for little bit
    Then maybe get some grub
    They thought the plan a good one
    But it didn't work out well
    Their faces both were recognised
    Someone gave a warning yell
    Next thing they were knowing
    They were running through the streets
    Evading angry citizens
    Performing flying feats
    They made it out beyond the Wag
    And scrambled for the hills
    They found a cave and hid inside
    Both fearful of the ills –
    That the Waggans would administer
    If they should happ to catch them
    To avoid this horrid outcome
    They found rocks and happ'ly stacked them
    Hidden by a wall of stones

That camouflaged their cave
They watched the world outside go dry
The sun then gave a wave.
In the morning, ambling up
Was a stranger cutting grass
He hoped to feed his emu
The day would be his last
The Kellyites got out their knives
Crept closer to the man
They sank their blades into his guts
Then saw his friends and ran
The dying man had screamed aloud
His friends had all come running
The Kellyites were out of there
T'ward a sunrise oh so stunning
Later on they ran into
A one-eyed shepherd man
Whom they seemed to be related to
Courtesy of clan

They told him 'bout the True Blue Way
    But he didn't want a bar
    And when he lay to have a sleep
    The Kellyites went too far
    Grabbing hold the shepherd's bow
    Taking off its tautened string
    One whispered to the shepherd man

On this yourself did bring
He plunged the object's pointed end
Right through the man's good eye
So deeply that it broke through skull
They laughed and said goodbye
Riding on, they came across
Some cheeky Mongrel Waggans
Killing one and seizing one
They proceeded after floggins
Ted heard all this and smile'd big
Then laughed most deep and loud
His men had done a goodly thing
And made their Captain proud.

A LITTLE BIT MORE VIOLENCE
PART II

Everyone was sayin'
    That they had killed a bloke
    But Ted said, 'Oi there's ten o' ya
    'This has gotta be a joke.
    'Alright, then, to prove it
    'Show us all your blade
    'I'll suss out in good order
    'By whom the kill was made.
    'This bloke here, I see it clear
    ''Twas him who made the kill
    'He stuck it deep in 'Zoozite gut
    'There's food on junior Bill.*
    In emulation of Captain Ted, the Kellyite had named his sword Bill Jr.

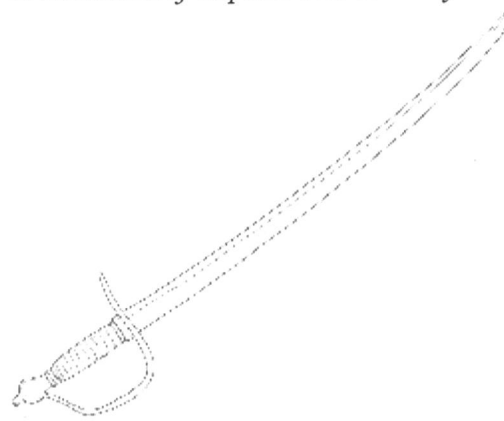

A LITTLE BIT MORE VIOLENCE
PART III
THE TALE OF BILLY BINOCULARS

The Captain was aggrieved by
    A certain female lyricist
    Whose songs were most contemptuous
    And encroaching on conspiracist
    To ease the poor old Captain's pain
    There went a blind old man
    Billy was his proper name
    He walked with groping hand
    Through the door of the artist's house
    And right up to her bed
    Billy, though he could not see
    Was capable, it must be said
    Sleeping on the woman's chest
    Was a cute and squishy baby
    Billy gently took it off her
    And didn't think that maybe –
    The kid might need a mother
    No Billy cared not about that
    He raised his sword and brought it down
    So deep it broke a slat
    The artist ably skewered
    Was an achievement, to be sure
    When Ted Kelly heard about it
    He just had to wiggle jaw
    'Billy the Blind, they call him
    'But I will tell youz that
    'His vision is twenty-twenty

'As good as a bloody cat!'
'We'll call him Billy Binoculars!'
A Kellyite voice rang out
This was in the clubhouse
After a quick head-bobbing bout.
With his brand new epithet
Billy really hit the town
Even visited the crime scene
And addressed a many frown
To the woman's grieving children
He said, 'Oi, all o' you.
'I'm the bloke that killed ya mutha
'Whatchaz gonna do?!'
Of course the kids did nothing
For though the man was blind
He was backed up by the Kellyites
And they *were not* of the mind –
To make themselves the victims
Of the members of Big Al's Team
Instead they moored their insults
And stifled primal scream.

PHILLIP'S CURIOUS CASE

To teach some nearby Mongrels
    The good ol' True Blue Way
    Ted sent some conquerisors
    With quotables to say
    Sometimes he went out with them
    And when he did, he took
    The wife who drew the winning stick
    Oh the lucky chook
    In canopies on wombats
    The wives did come along
    And from their private boxes
    They cheered the soldiers on

The sound they made one certain day

Was not of cheering kind
But a groan most sympathetic
For a reason you'll now find:
Phillip was a Kellyite
Who happily conquerised
But hapt to miss an enemy
And found himself surprised
'Stabbed ma bloody self, I did
'In the flamin' guts
'Lucky it wasn't lower
'Coulda cut off both ma nuts.'
The bright side did not hold him long
Unless one counts Upstairs
The shining light that opened up
Grabbed Phil most unawares
Suicide, to a Kellyite
Is a roastable offence
The person who performs it
Gets a Hellish consequence
So now there was the question
Of what had hapt to Phil
'Did he make it up to Paradise
'Or is he down in Hill?'*
*That question was asked by a Kiwi convert to the True Blue Way.
Ted made the declaration
That Phillip's sheet was clean
It wasn't flat-out suicide
Conquerising, he had been
The principle here established
Would echo through the ages
The Kellyites often use it
To supplement their rages
Effectively, what the edict means
Is that one's self-termination
Will take one off to Paradise...

If dinting Mongrel population.
This explains the many fireworks
That erupt across the earth
And how Kellyites with flying limbs
Can have faces showing mirth.

SIGHTS ON WAGGA

Not a great deal happened
    For several months thereafter
    There was a fight at a local drinking hole
    And a skirmish with some farmers
    In the hacienda
    In the office where Ted worked
    He opened up a desk drawer
    To have his good self perked
    His walls, it will be noted
    Are all devoid of pictures
    Ted Kelly hated images
    Even says so in his scriptures
    This is why the Kellyites
    Make very little art
    Images soak up Big Al's due
    'Would ya give him half your heart?'
    But Teddy kept a picture
    That reminded him of the Wag
    Freddy, he had brought it
    On the migratory slog
    It was a Wanted poster
    That had Ted Kelly's face
    And *Reward of hundred camels*
    For whoever ends our chase.

The Waggans they had set a price
    On Captain Kelly's head
    To get him off their dusty streets
    Alive or pref'rably dead
    For reasons one can't penetrate
    The sentiment made Ted grateful
    Wagga Wagga Wagga...Wagga Wagga
    Was a town he held a flame for
    Deeply did he want to go
    And walk again its streets
    And barrack at the local Pub
    And taste its famous meats
    But the Waggans did not want this
    Oh my goodness no
    If the Captain stepped within the town
    My there'd be a show

But the desire was a strong one
Like a river underground
And it pushed the Cap so greatly
A way must sure be found
He went down to the clubhouse
And gave a lucid speech
Its title, it was:
Wagga, oh so within reach
He said they'd make a Pub Crawl
As many as they could
And why should they all do this?
Because we bloomin' should!
Seven-hundred Kellyites
Set out from Wangaratta
Destined for the Waggan Pub
On a Crawl of serious matter
The Waggans heard about it
And raised a quick defence
Quickly they did head out
And warnings did commence.
'Step no bloody further
'You flamin' Kellyites
'Make your move 'n' re-learn
'We Waggans thrive on fights.'
'Calm your roos and hear the news,'
Said the envoy sent by Ted
'We haven't come to have a blue
'So get that in your head.'
The Waggans heard the Team's desire
And said, 'Nuh-uht, no way
'The Wag you aren't attaining
'Right now or *any* day.'
A bit of back-and-forthing
Proceeded to ensue
The envoy went back Team-ward

With a paper sheet or two.
'They asked us for a treaty,'
Is what the envoy said,
'I told 'em I would say no thing
'Without consulting Ted.'
Wayne was listening closely
As this meeting tooketh place
His blood pressure was rising
He was crimson in the face
'Outrageous!' he then shouted
'They can keep their poxy treaty
'A deal with all those Mongrels
'Has the value of graffiti!
'The True Blue Way is overhead
'They don't deserve to touch it
'Tell 'em they can bugger off
'The Team's insulted mucheth!'
Ted raised a hand and calmed him down
'Hang on, Waynie boy
'Remember what Al said to me
'In regard to plan and ploy?
'They plot and scheme against ya, Ted
'But I plot 'n' scheme 'gainst them
'So therefore just deal calmly
'Alone just leaveth them.
'But only for a little while
''Cause Big Al is pullin' strings.
'Has someone got some red ink?
'I might cross out certain things.'
Redacted was the treaty
Return'd to the Wags
Who looked at it most closely
Thinking, *Lord, he's lost his cogs*
'If we thought Ted a Spokesman
'We'd all have nought to say

'But all be bobbin' with ya
'Throughout the live-long day
'Hence we shall not sign it
'This document you've got
'It's little more than gobble-gook
'A stack o' bloomin' rot.'
Back and forth the papers went
Till a settlement was made
War would be a no-go
For duration of decade
But in a year the Kellyites
Could rock up and visit town
They could stay three days and then get out
Or their pants'd be pulled down.

CHEER UP, FELLAS...

As the Captain and his many men
    Turned and headed for their homes
    Ted spoke with force and brevity
    To address the many moans
    'Don't worry men, we've got ourselves
    'An outcome to be glad about
    'The treaty with the Waggans
    'Is a step-up, let us shout!
    'This day we are regarded
    'As a force to be reckoned with
    'That the Wags negotiated
    'Means the Team is gettin' big
    'And this'll boost the confidence
    'Of people on the fence
    'To join a mighty Team, ya see
    'Is a choice of common sense.
    'If your bottom lips are hangin' low
    'Might I do some heavy lifting?
    'It seems the Angel Ferdy
    'Just did some vision-gifting.'
    'Those who did not come with us
    'On this prestigious Crawl
    'Shall not partake of future spoils
    'But Lord they'll get a brawl
    'I see a war is coming
    ''Gainst people of mighty strength
    'We'll fight until they all submit
    'No matter the battle's length
    'The many who endure it
    'Big Al will treat 'em nice
    'But those who turn away from it
    'Will pay a costly price.'

A LITTLE BIT MORE VIOLENCE
PART IV

Several fellas fronted up
    To pay the Wang a visit
    Their bellies started rumbling
    Soon they all were convalescent
    Ted walked around and had a look
    And gave his diagnosis
    Said it wasn't Haemmorhoidal
    Or cellular mitosis
    'I know just what'll fix yaz,'
    Said good ol' Captain Ted
    'A decent drink o' cattle pee
    'And some milk, that it ferment.'
    The men all staggered out of town
    And found a lonely drover
    Tending to his cattle
    Near a windmill knock'd over
    They asked if he might kindly grant
    Permission to use their cows
    That their urine and their lactate
    Might help to calm one's bowels
    'No worries, gents,' the man replied
    'In fact I'll help yaz out
    'I'll go and get the stuff ya need
    'I' got cup and even spout.'
    The man returned, the men all drank
    In time the men improved
    And then to show their gratitude
    They had their nurse removed
    The meaning of that statement is

They killed him quick and fast
Then nicked the poor bloke's cattle
And left him in the past.
Ted heard all this and then said, 'What!?
'Those cheeky rotten ratbags!
'Find 'em boys and bring 'em back
'We'll use 'em all as box-bags.'
By noon the Kellyites had the men
They brought them back to Ted
Who said to gouge out all their eyes
With pokers hot and red
'As well as that cut off their hands
'And also take their feet
'Dump 'em onto sharpened rocks
'The sun'll cook 'em just like meat.'

ARAYONGA

'Alright blokes, let's saddle up
    'We have a new objective
    'The town of Arayonga
    'Shall experience our collective
    'We have no need of camping out
    'To hear a morning yodel
    'This town, we know, is 'Zoozite-filled
    'Unfamiliar with our modal
    'But that won't be for very long
    'In a quick amount o' time
    'They'll all be shoutin' Al's the best
    'Or face a painful fine.'
    Eighteen-hundred Kellyites
    Set out for Arayonga
    A hundred-and-fifty kays away
    Though the heat made it feel longer
    They waited for the sun to rise
    Heard no call to bob one's head
    And that was deemed permission
    To rob the Mongrels dead
    Ted climbed a roo and gave a speech
    His men were all enthused
    They found themselves all itching
    For their weapons to be used
    'When we ride against a nation
    'Which hath ignored our warning
    'It will find that it is in for
    'A *very* terrible morning!
    'So come on boys, Big Al's the best
    'Arayonga is destroyed
    'Let's go and kill some Mongrels
    'May our swords all be employed!'

As well as swords, they brought their guns
And with them happ'ly shot
The farmers and the workers
And the people who forgot –
'That Ted Kelly writes the rules round here
'Big Al he is the best
'The True Blue Way is paramount
'Disbelieve, we'll stab your chest!'
The people of the town all fled
As the Team-mates smashed and looted
A 'Zoozite mayor named Dennis
Armoured-up and much refuted –
The Kellyite assertion
That certain things were owed
He swung a sword and fought real well
Till a fatal blow was blowed

And then of course his neck was chopped
His head was lifted high
The mayor of Arayonga
Was a trophy price'd high
So too were all the sheilas
The attractive ones, anyway
They were caught and then distributed
Till Ted had things to say
'Hey all youz remember
'What Big Al said to me
'The choosing of the wives you like
'First goes to Captain Teddy
'And Teddy, he likes that one
'Who has got her now?

'I'll trade for two of her cousins
'Maybe even add a cow.'
The deal was made, the girl was Ted's
He chucked her in a tent
Saying, 'I'll be back in later
'Show ya how to pay your rent.'
Of course the Captain was a gentlemen
He lived by certain rules
On the siege of Arayonga
He made it clear for fools:
'We Kellyites impose ourselves
'Not on bleeding women
'If they're On the Rag, we're off 'em
'Our seeds shall not be swimmin'
'And by the way I might digress
'To attend a bygone matter
'*Coitus interruptus*
''Tis better than the latter –
'And by the "latter," what I mean
'Is the idea putteth forth:
'To cut off one's own pee wee flute
'To avoideth intercourth.
''Cause on a long-range mission
''Tis hard, I must acknowledge
'To go without one's buxom wife
'And get no morning porridge.*
* Porridge was a euphemism for love.
'But the price-of-slave goes down a bit
'If their belly starts to bulge
'So to blast your merry buckshot
'At the ground, problem solved!
'All of that I understand
'But I do advise against it
''Cause if Big Al wants a soul to be
'It shall be, let's not prevenst it

'So here I do by certify
'The law of three-day marriage
'To alleviate the carnal urge
'That gives slave a baby carriage.
''Cause your slaves have all got things to do
'They cannot be detained
'By the drawn-out inconvenience
'Of a child that need be trained
'So summing up, let's say it clear
'Don't slip it to your slave
'But get yourself a three-day-wife
'So much trouble it'll save!*

*Not all present-day Kellyites believe in three-day marriages. Some maintain that Ted told Freddy he had changed his mind about them.

'But back on track we need to be
'Where was I? Ohr yes there
'It seems I've only one thing more
'I say it 'cause I care.
'In regard to captive women
'If they happen to be preggers
'Don't force oneself upon them
'Till they've birthed their little beggars.'
With that, Ted concluded
And headed for his tent
But was stopped by several Team-mates
Who had grievances to vent
'Behold the spoils surrounding
'Low they seem to be
'Surely there is more here
'Wherever could it be?"
A 'Zooite man was push'd forth
In fact he hapt to be
The husband of the Looker
Now the Captain's property
His name was Keith, and it was said

He knew where treasure be
Keith said he knew but nothing
A simple man was he
But someone spoke up quietly
Saying Keithie had been seen
Hanging round some ruins
'Go there n' sweep 'em clean.'
Sure enough they went there
And found a treasure chest
They opened it and wanted more
So built a fire on Keithie's chest

They tortured him until he reached
    For the handle of death's door
    Keithie he said nothing
    Ted said, 'Alright men, no more.'
    Keith was handed over
    To a Kellyite bereaved
    The battle killed his brother
    His sword it was unsheathed
    He cut off Keithie's Mongrel head
    And did it with delight

'One does not trifle with Al's Team.
''Gainst us ya should not fight.'

THE OATIS TAX
(STILL IN ARAYONGA)

A man not previously mentioned
    Was Ted's slave, named Billy Lee
    He had hold of some 'Zoozite chicks
    And was leading them hastily
    Tactlessly he walked past
    The bodies of their spouses
    The women screamed like demon hags
    Or kids in burning houses
    'Billy Lee ya bloody fool
    'Have ya got bloody no heart
    'Get those she-devils away from me
    'That'll be a bloody start.
    'I'm tryin' to use ma brain, y'see
    ''Cause here I'm lookin' round
    'Seein' that certain opportunities
    'Might well'a just been found.
    'The 'Zoos of Arayonga
    'Appear quite well endowed
    'They've got seed and they've got implement
    'I'm sure they'll make us proud.
    'Don't worry all you farmers
    ''Cause we're not gonna kill ya
    'Not if youz all get to work
    'All we'll do is bill ya.
    'If all you 'Zoozites work the land
    'And tend your happy fields
    'Then we'll show up biannual
    'To partake of all your yields.
    'This tax I've just invented

'Deserves a proper title
'I believe I'll call it *Oatis**
'Think of wild oats and their cycle!'
*I hope youz got the subtext
*But it yes rather vague
*I'd recommend a scholar
*If the play on word doth plague.
* And if it plagues ye endless
*Give up and don't look back
*Wasn't very clever
*Let's all stay on track.
'Alright then, let's get to work
'On fillin' up our guts
'Someone start the barbeque
'Who's good at shellin' nuts?'

THAT NIGHT...

Collapsed around a campfire
    Exhausted by the day
    The Kellyites ate most avidly
    And toasted loud The Way

Till Teddy had a bite of meat
    And quickly spat it out
    'What the bloody bulldust!'
    He said by way of shout
    'Someone's tried to poison me
    'I taste it in this meat
    'Grab the chef and bring 'em ere
    'The bugger will be beat!'
    Shuffled to the front of mob
    Came an ancient wizened lady
    Who addressed the charge most honestly
    Said she'd even stirred the gravy
    Lost for words, Ted looked at her
    Then got hold of his tongue
    'Why, ya geriatric bag?
    'What've *I* ever done?'
    'Ya killed me bloody family

'So I put poison in your dinner
'If *really* you're a Spokesman
'Then you'll come out a winner

'A king would fall, like those blokes there
     'They're clutchin' guts and sinkin'
     'But a man who's backed by the Bloke Upstairs
     'He'd survive it, goes ma thinkin'.'
     Implicit was the challenge
     Which one of them was Ted?
     A Spokesman who would see it out
     Or a bloke who'd wind up dead?

THE NEXT MORNING...

Ted felt he gave the answer
    When he lived throughout the night
    He called himself the victor
    In the Battle of the Bite
    And true was he delighted
    When some visitors swung around
    Coming from a nearby town
    To bow and touch the ground
    Big Al's Team had won their hearts
    Or perhaps their adrenal glands
    They pledged themselves to Teddy's whims
    And offered all their hands
    Ted said, 'Alright you mob
    'For now I'll let yaz be
    'Go back home and till your ground
    'In time you'll hear from me
    'The Oatis tax is coming
    'For it you must prepare
    'And there are some stipulations
    'Attendant, I'll now share:
    'Ye shall be known as Dhummies.
    'And live a certain way
    'Your houses can't be higher
    'Than a Kellyite's, I do say
    'And neither can you testify
    'Against a True Blue member
    'The Oatis tax'll be fifty percent
    'Of annual earnings, due november
    'Alright then, let's grab our roos
    'And bounce on out of here
    'I'll send a tax collector
    'Treat him nice and feel no fear.' *

The first tax collector had his neck broken and was thrown down a well.

THE RETURN TO WANGARATTA

On the Wangward journey
    Several episodes tooketh place
    In one a slave named Neville
    Copped a bullet in the face
    At first he was a martyr
    But then on closer look
    Nev wore a spiffy jacket
    From the spoils it had been took!

'Nifty bloody Neville
    'Is a thief, it is apparent
    'Therefore he is now burning
    'For behaviour most aberrant.
    'The corpse of Nifty Neville
    'Makes a principle come to life:
    'Those with nimble fingers
    'Will earn eternal strife!'
    The secondary episode

Relates to Honeymoon
When the captive girl in Teddy's tent
No doubt was made to swoon.
Outside the tent that raucous night
There stood a Kellyite
"Faithful and not eavesdropping"
He was ready for a fight
"'Cause call me crazy, Captain Ted
'But true it seems to me
'Your new girl might be dangerous
'On account of history
'Only just now yesterday
'Did we put to death her folk
'She might not have forgotten that
'Truly, it's no joke
'Even in a dainty hand
'A blade can conjure grief
'If no one's there to help ya
'You're done-for's my belief.'
Ted thanked the man and blessed him
Then went inside his tent
One presumes Ted had a thrilling time
(Risking life, is what is meant).

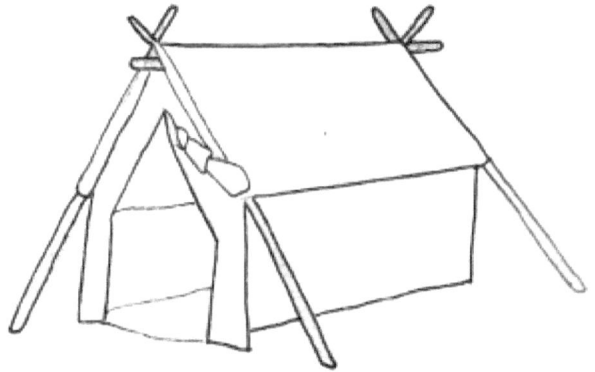

IN THE WANG...

On arrival they all dumped the goods
    And counted up their treasure
    'The pile is most impressive,'
    Said a man with tape'd measure
    Ted selected eighteen men
    To allocate the loot
    A ratio was established
    Ted thought it pretty beaut
    Three shares went to the cavalry-men
    Who rode the kangaroos
    While one share went to the foot soldiers
    Who'd worn out all their shoes.

As all this was taking place

A Refo name of Brett
Sidled up to Ted and said,
'Hey Captain, got a sec?
'I wonder might I head on back
'To Wagga, for a reason
'See people owe me cash, and well
'To get it, they need squeezin'
'But pressure I don't wanna give
'So if it's alright with you
'Mind if I maybe tell a fib
'Or maybe even two?'
Captain Ted held out his hands
And said, 'Oh Bretty Brett
'*War, it is deceit*, I've said
'That idea you have to get.
'Of course you can, you cheeky boy
'Head back to good ol' Wag
'Tell as many fibs as needeth be
'If it gets ya what ya want
'If a person is a Mongrel
'Then see the truth as malleable
'You can twist it, you can turn it
'And shape it till it's carryable
'Give to them what they want to have
'And give it to 'em good
'They are the worstest creatures
'Far less valuable than wood.'
Brett hurried off to Wagga
A smile upon his face
And there disseminated
A lie, with poise and grace

'The Battle of Arayonga
　'Fared poorly for Ted Kelly
　'The man is now a prisoner
　'And oh so ever smelly.'
　A cheer arose in Wagga Town
　And the Waggans had no clue
　That Brett was now a Kellyite
　So his cash he did accrue
　Under breath he said some words
　Contemptuous of the people
　Because it rhymed it well aligned
　With Ted Kelly's stated principle:
　'Insult the Mongrels with your poems
　''Cause Ferdy's got your back
　'He'll be there to protect you
　'So go on, have a crack.'*
　*Conquerisors of the Pen and the Word are subjects worthy of study.

THE BOB CHANGE

Deep in the Captain's bosom
    There burned a passionate flame
    It longed for a certain home-town
    Wagga was its name

To illuminate the fondness
    That Teddy felt for Wag
    Learn of how he changed the rules
    Of the direction one must bog*
    *Bog. Verb. Aussie slang. Meaning: to defecate.
    Did the narrator use the proper word
    Did he mean to say head *bob?*
    Negative, is the answer
    The word correct is *bog.*
    But *bob* is strong related

And it was change'd too
"A quick recalibration"
Had foot in "correct shoe"
If one has paid attention
One might now be aware
The Kellyites bobbed to 'Brusalem
A city far and fair
But this all changed one historic day
When Teddy spoke up loud
It happened in the clubhouse
Where he had a decent crowd
The men had gone to bob their heads
But the Captain raised a hand
Saying, 'Al made alterations
'To the laws of all this land
'Formerly we bobbed our heads
'Toward ol' Canny Brue
'But now we bob to Wagga
'You all know what to do!'
Murmurs rose and eyebrows too
People smirked and looked around
Why the sudden change, ol' mate?
An answer have ye found?
It seems a mite convenient
To part with stated aim
When those pesky Mongrel 'Zoozites
All did fail to sign their name
Ted Kelly he was not a man
Whom one could call a 'tard
These mumblings and these grumblings
Did not hit him very hard:
He had an answer line'd up
He gave no hesitations
He calmed the gathered Kellyites
And assuaged their protestations

'The fools among the people
'Will say, *Why the hell's it changed?*
'We was bobbin' toward 'Brusalem
'And had it all arranged
'Ask not me, but ask of Al
'He's the one that makes the choices
'He's given me a message
'Please lower all your voices
'To Al belongs the east and west
'He guides whoever he pleases
'Toward a Way so ever straight
'So bob and make some breezes!
'And all o' youz please dwell upon
'The direction of those winds
'They're blowin' forth to Wagga now
'May I see no head that spins.'
They nodded all together
The Family, The Gang
The Team of firm believers
In the message Ted had brang
And now we come to bogging
For which the Captain made a law
There were certain stipulations
One simply can't ignore
''Tis forbidden most acutely
'To pÜÜp or pee in line
'With the sacred town of Wagga
'To its left or right is fine
'T'ward the Wag or 'way from
'Both are contraband
'Regardless of how busting
'I'm sure you understand.
'So bob one way and bog another
'Do your part for one and all
'Steel your necks and grit your teeth

'We'll bob ourselves a squall!'

THE TEMPORARY RETURN TO WAGGA

A year had passed since they'd met the Wags
    And signed a humble treaty
    It was now the time to hit the town
    Be the weather good or sleety
    Packing up and heading out
    They made the Wagward trip
    An excitement most electric
    Had them strongly in its grip.
    Outside the town they pause'd brief
    Ted beheld the Wag and sighed
    Then said, 'Oi where's that donkey
    'It's been bloody prophesied –
    'That the bloke who is the main event
    'Will come to town on colt
    'Bloody hold it properly would yaz
    'It looks about to bolt.'

Ted rode the donkey into Wag
  He waved at passersby
  A Kellyite out in front of him
  Announce'd with a cry:
  'Get out the way ya Mongrels!
  'Or we'll cut off your head!
  'Friend we shall remove from friend!
  'Yaz heard what I just said!'
  Stopping at the famous Pub
  Ted hopped down off his donkey
  The moment so significant
  He felt a fraction wonky
  Many years had it been
  Since being in this place
  He had to wipe a bulging tear
  Running down his face.

MEMORIES...

Embedded in the cornerstone
    Of Ted's beloved Pub
    There was in fact a moon rock
    Ted gave the thing a rub

More than that, he kissed it
    Several times, in fact
    He walked a lap and leaned in close
    In joy the man was wrapt.
    Fondly he remembered
    The time he'd help to plant it
    He'd solved a growing clan dispute
    'Bout the family to be granted –
    The honour of re-cementing
    The famous lunar stone
    At the end of a big reno

In which a blue had nearly blown
But Teddy, he had solved it
By simply walking past
The Aussies all said, 'You there!
'Come here and do it fast
'There's twelve of us here families
'And we each desire the honour
'Of puttin' back the moon rock
'Make your choice; who is gonna?'
Teddy was most tactful
He said to put it down
'Right there upon me jacket
'Yeht, now spin it round
'Now all of us'll lift it
'See we're doin' it all together
'No one is excluded
'Hey how about this weather?'
While they were distracted
By looking at the sky
Teddy grabbed the moon rock
And lifted it real high
Careful he did set it
In the cement of cornerstone
When all the Aussies looked again
They cringed and loudly groaned
That no one else had got the gift
Of being the one to do it
Meant the Aussies were forgiving
Of Ted Kelly, and he knew it
So happily he'd walked away
Having solved a fight a'brewing
Two camels he saluted
Cud they were a'chewing

BACK TO IT...

Consider now the treaty
    Which let Teddy stay three days
    He tried to draw it out a bit
    But Mayor Morry said, *No ways.*
    The Waggans were behind him
    They were all of single mind:
    Collect your things, please, Captain
    The exit you'll now find.
    Roos they were a'saddled
    And Wombats loaded up
    Big Al's Team set off for Wang
    Having happ'ly filled their cup.

FIGHTENOUS MUTHAS

Annoyingly, the treaty
    Emphasised explicitly
    A ban on war for ten long years
    The Team was getting fidgety
    Ted found the boys an outlet
    When checkin' out the maps
    'Get a load of all the Britons
    ''N where they hang their caps.'
    The Kelly Gang was growing large
    Its muscle needed flexing
    A fight with Mongrel Britons
    Would see toughness get a testing
    He sent three-thousand soldiers
    To give the Brits a beating
    But superior organisation
    Had the Team-mates greatly bleeding
    Those who made it out alive
    Were scorn'd for the act
    That they had not died while conquerising
    Made them chickens, that was fact
    Thrown in their direction
    Were many kinds of poo
    The men all had to wear it
    What else could they do?
    The Captain gained a full report
    Of all that had taken place
    In spite of Al's directive
    There was grief upon his face*
    *Ted said those who die in the act of conquerising should not be mourned
excessively.

'Every man who battled
'And promptly lost his spirit
'Went skyward t'ward the Big P
'On beds of gold; let's hear it –

'For every single martyr
    'Except for old mate Daniel
    'Apparently he flinch'd
    'What a cocker spaniel!
    ''Cause 'member boys, one should not cringe
    'When running into fight
    'Meagre are the benefits
    'If ya let 'em see your fright
    'Your beds of gold will turn away
    'As they slow on their approach
    'This, my jolly comrades
    'Is Big Al's firm reproach
    'And all-you out there chuckin' poo
    'At these service-men returning

'They're stockin'-up far more reward
'Than what all *youz* are earning
'Cause those who fight with wealth and lives
'Outrank those who stay at home
'Excluded are the disabled
'Let 'em lie on beds of foam.*

This must be a transliteration error, as foam was not invented for at least another thousand years.

'Right now we're on a topic
'That lives deep inside my chest
'Y'might not like to battle
'But it's clearly for your best
"Cause Allan loves a solid wall
'Made of soldiers grouped together
'And those who fighteth for his cause
'He loves 'em even better.
'And oohp, just got a message
'From Ferdy, and what he says
'Is that those who died in battle
'Left the Earth at Al's behest
'See Big Al he had planned it
"Cause some were meant to die
'And others they were meant to live
'Hence they did not say goodbye.'

MOZZA

A fact not previously mentioned
    Is that Mayor Morry had a child
    Several of them, rather
    And one did something wild
    She married Captain Kelly
    And moved off to the Wang
    Geraldine, her name was
    Her phone, it rarely rang
    For silence was her greatest friend
    And this might half explain
    Why Mozza, when he visited
    Was treated with disdain
    'I thought I'd swing on by your house
    'And visit me young daughter
    'How are ya Geraldeenie
    'Bein' treated as ya oughta?
    'As well as that I've come around
    'To have some words with Ted
    'He's been stirrin' up some trouble
    'With some allies, it's been said.
    'Our treaty yes allows it
    'Alliances, they are fine
    'But for the sake of curiosity
    'I'd like to learn Ted's mind
    'Will Team-mates soon be loan'd
    'To help out in a fight
    'I'll just sit on this carpet
    'OOOH, I got a fright!'
    The reason Moz got frightened
    Is 'cause Geraldine did a dive
    Snatched the carpet that he'd aimed for
    Then jumped up most alive

'This carpet shan't be sullied by
'My unclean Mongrel father
'Defile'd it will not be
'Dead I would be rather.
'Ted Kelly, he has sat on it
'Thus need it to be stated
''Tis a highly-prize'd artefact
'One easily deem'd sacred.'
'Righto then,' said Mozza
Standing to his feet
'I shall tracketh down your husband
'And see if me he'll meet.'
Morry left the hacienda
And looked about for Ted
He was told Ted would not see him
No other words were said.
The question was asked of Bazza
And then of good ol' Wayne
Then Freddy copped it squarely
The answer was the same.
'The Captain will not see you
'I shan't speak on his behalf
'Go away ya Mongrel
'Or I will start to laugh.'
Mayor Morry spat upon the dust
Then climbed atop his roo
'Catcha later Wangaratta
'With you I am most through.'
He hopped away that autumn day
Never looking back
And had zero intuitions
Ted was planning an attack.

WAGGA HERE WE COME

All across the continent
    Ted had Kellyites
    And now he called upon them
    For the biggest of all fights.
    Ten-thousand men from all around
    Took weapons into hand
    They put on shoes and climbed their roos
    And travelled 'cross the land
    The Gang was now a big one
    A swelling fearsome army
    A dark and crackling storm cloud
    That made Australia balmy
    Watch it treading over earth
    Its members all excited
    Heading for the nexus
    Where the barrack lines united
    Destiny was edging close
    The Captain he could feel it
    Wagga would be his quite soon
    The deal was almost seal'd
    As to be expected
    He gave a rousing speech
    'Come on boys, let's make some noise
    'Wagga is in reach!
    'And do you need reminding
    'Of how the world's divided
    'There are Team-mates, there are Mongrels
    'Two species un-collided
    'With them we shall not marry
    'We're of a different crew
    'In the House of War they live
    'While we live in True Blue!

'In their hearts we'll striketh fear
'Cut off their Mongrel noggins
'Surround 'em with every ambush
''N give 'em lots o' floggins.
''Cause those who war against Big Al
'Of harm they are deserving
'Truly we shall make 'em bleed
''Cause Allan's who we're serving!
'The Team of Truth is what we are
'And if we go unchosen
'We'll wage a vicious battle
'Till Hell is all but frozen
'Alright then, let's carry on
'The Wag's our destination
'Let's find some jolly Mongrels
'Who need decapitation!'
A hitch occurred when someone sped
Beyond the marching Gang
In his knapsack was a letter:
A written warning clang
But beans were spilled, the man was grabbed
And brought before the Captain
Had the man not served at Glendam
Burial shroud he woulda been wrapped in
Allowed to keep his head, he was
And for that he was quite grateful
'But when it comes to meal times, mate
'You'll be last to get a plate-full!'
Mayor Morry heard the Kellyites
Were heading for the town
So bounced on out and found their camp
Deeply did he frown
'Good lord they are quite numerous
'And formidable in strength,'
He said while twisting spyglass

To adjust its focal length
'What on earth are we to do
'Us unprepare'd Waggans
'It looks as though we're in for
'Unmitigated floggins.'
Mayor Morry did not know it
But he was spotted by a scout
And to a small contingent
The Kellyite sang out
In *no* time Moz was rounded up
And brought to Teddy's tent
The Captain had his thongs off
And to his bed he went
Wayne was there and sure enough
He wanted Mozza dead
'Come one, Cap, let's get it done
'I'll cut off his Mongrel head.'
But the Captain yawned and shook his own
Saying, 'Nah come back tomorrow.
'Already I am half asleep
'For that, please take my sorrow.'
Mayor Morry took it with a smile
Not crafty, but of relief
Then went to find a quiet spot
To have a slumber brief
When in time the sun arose
Climbing from its muddy pool*
Mozza straightened out his shirt
And gripped his sharpest tool
Ted Kelly avowed that the sun, when setting, sinks into a pool of mud.
Charm, it was, that aided him
In all of his pursuits
It helped him forge connections
That put him in cahoots –
With Waggan luminaries

(Hence how he'd been elected)
So now he'd have to bung it on
To keep neck from being dissected
Ted Kelly was having breakfast
When Moz knocked upon his door
The sound was greatly muted
It was a tent flap, nothing more
'Come in, Moz, and have a seat,'
The Captain said politely
'I'm sure you've things to tell me
'Make it quick, I'm scheduled tightly
'Or cutting the preamble
'I'll come right out and ask it:
'Ya ready now to chuck your eggs
'In the Kellyites' basket?'
Mayor Morry drew a tired breath
And said, 'Ya know what?'
'I thought there was a Bloke Upstairs
''Side from Al, but apparently not.
'Otherwise he woulda spoken up
'But here's me sittin' now
'With Captain Ted at breakfast-time
'Wipin' off me brow.'
'That ya *should* be doing,'
Said Ted, with pointed butter knife
''Cause if ya do not join the Team
'Mozza, you will lose your life
'Submit right now and testify
'*There's no else Upstairs*
'*Al's the only Bloke above*
'*And Ted's his man, I swears.*
'Otherwise ya lose your head
'And it *will* be hard to find
'Re-attaching them is challenging
'I'm sure your kids will find.'

'When it's put like *that*,' said the Mayor of Wag
'It really does yes seem
'The smartest thing for me to do
'Is sign up to the Team.'
Ted clapped his hands and rubbed them
In tiny little circlets
And offered his new Team-mate
A plate of tasty pikelets
'The first thing you can do, ol' Moz
'Is stand upon a hill
'And watch our righteous army
'Flooding in to make a kill
'However, let me quickly add
'There be no need of slaughter
'If all the Mongrel Waggans
'Simply do the things they oughta:
'Sign their names and join the Team
'And say that I'm their Captain
'Do all this, there'll be no fuss
'A good time they'll be havin'.
'So head on out and spread the word
'Tell 'em Captain Ted is coming
'If they chance to not-believe ya
'Just say, *Listen for the drumming.*'

MOZ TO THE WAG...

Mayor Morry ate his pikelets
    Then did as he was told
    Allowed to keep his titles
    He'd been welcomed to the fold
    He called a general meeting
    The Waggans did attend
    He advised against resistance
    Saying, 'Ted is now ma friend.'
    Giving up a shy salute
    He left the men to talk
    Then up the required mountain
    The Mayor began his walk
    When standing on the top of it
    He looked out across the flats
    A man of lesser courage
    Woulda dropped some patty splats
    From the north and from the south
    Ten-thousand arm'd men
    Were flooding t'ward the valley
    Found by Captain Abraham
    Wagga was surrounded
    But this the Mayor had known
    There was nothing for a man to do
    But stand and watch and groan.
    Thirteen blokes resisted
    When the Kellyites came to town
    Quickly they all met their end
    Their pants not stain'd brown
    Everybody else, though
    Would have to do some washing
    Having heeded Teddy's messengers
    In their homes they were a'squashing

Ted bounced along the dusty streets
And fronted to the Pub
Dropping off his kangaroo
He gave its nose a rub
Fondly he remembered
His soapbox and old Beryl
And the times when he and Bazza
Taught the Way till throats were sterile
He looked ahead and squinted at
The Pub's old wooden door
Thinking how he'd not been in there
For ten good years or more
He shouted out, 'Who's got the key?!
Quick smart it was produced
Ted walked toward the doorway
Thinking, *My, it has reduced*
Or maybe I've got taller
Given now I am the Cap
He made it to the wooden door
Out of habit, gave a rap
Swatting at his silliness
He poke'd in the key
Turned the handle, pushed the door
And looked inside to see –

An interior ever dusty
    Filled with sundry paraphernalia
    Collected from all kinds of teams
    Scattered right across Australia
    'Smash it, boys,' is what Ted said
    To Wayne and nephew Fred
    'Smash it all and grind it down
    'I wanna see it all look dead.'
    Ted grabbed hold of a sculpture
    And threw it at the floor
    It shattered into pieces
    His men went tooth and claw –
    Smashing, bashing, throwing
    All the things of ancient teams
    So loud that every Waggan
    Would have heard their laughing screams

They had the rubble sweep'd up
By compliant Waggan kids
'Now the Pub is ready
'To be used as Big Al bids.
''Cause 'memba, all you cheeky lot
'The other teams are gone
'Now there's just the Kelly Gang
'The Age of Al is born.
'And all teamish paraphernalia
'Is outlawed straightaway
'Vengeance as well as haemo cash
'Has also seen its day.'

ALTHOUGH...

Before that law was written in
    Ted settled several scores
    By happ'ly executing
    Mongrel Wags with flappin' maws
    This included various satirists
    And a former secretary;
    A man of keenest insult;
    And politicians labelled *wary*
    After doing seven Pub laps
    Touching moon rock every time
    Ted dusted off a chair and sat
    Before him formed a line
    And to him came the Waggans
    The men, and then the women
    All giving their allegiance
    Their enthusiasm brimmin'
    The wealthy chook who'd freed her slave
    In exchange for killing Hame
    Even did a curtsy
    And toasted Teddy's fame
    Presumably she looked morose
    Ted said, 'Don't kill your kids.'
    She said, 'They're dead already
    'Bloody Glendam did Al's bids.'
    Owing to Ted's holiness
    He couldn't hold her hand
    As she pledge'd her allegiance
    To Big Al and his band
    He got young Wayne to do it
    (And Wayne he did it well)
    Then Ted announced that Wagga
    'Is sacred, can't you tell?

'This is the Holy City
'And to it all should come
'Long as you're a Kellyite
'If you're not, kiss ma bum
'And bloody stay away from
'This reverential site
'Mongrels are not welcome here
'Try to risk it, brave a fight.
'But hey there everybody
'For your slaves I have a word:
'Sign your name and join the Team
'Your freedom you'll have earned.'
(Were it not that everyone
(Who signs their name True Blue
(Is held to be a slave of Al
(Ted would have spoken true
(In fact he'd be considered
(The foremost abolitionist
(Instead of the less flattering term:
(An equivocating conditionalist.
(Best is that condition seen
(In regard to holding tight
(To one's cheeky human chattel
(Which is hoping to make flight
(Ted scribbled in a loophole
(To help retain one's slaves:
(*Dispute the slave's commitment*
(*To the Gang and all its ways*).
Dusted, done, and kicking back
Ted looked around most pensive
He'd achieved his great ambition
Now he'd need a *new* offensive.

THE KING OF AUSTRALIA

Scattered throughout the continent
    Were Aussies much concern'd
    They watched the growth of Big Al's Team
    For former times they yearn'd
    Creating coalitions
    They met and made a decision
    Then counted up their numbers
    And set out on a vital mission
    Strong within their tribal mind
    Was a somber realisation:
    If the Captain stayed upon his perch
    He'd be king of all the nation
    The fire that was the Kellyites
    Was raging across the land
    Leaving peaceful thriving townships
    All desolate and damned
    The worst thing was the head bob
    It was spreading like a sickness
    A virus oh so virulent
    Trapped in domes of ultra thickness
    Truly it was hard to watch
    This head bob taking hold
    'To watch an upright person bend...
    'Makes your gizzards all go cold.'
    And to hear it be encouraged
    By people whom one knew;
    Who in the past had used their brains
    But now all seemed to spew:
    'Look around and look real close
    'To see who's bobbin' low
    'Perhaps it isn't low enough
    'They have much more to go

'If that's the case then push 'em down
'Or notify authorities
'The head bob must be done just right
'No exceptions for minorities!'
The Mongrel Coalition
As henceforth we shall know it
Was surprisingly well organised
And Ted he did not know it
Marching out to meet it
With twelve-thousand Kellyites
They all looked upon the army
And many got the frights
'Where yaz bloody goin'!'
Screamed Teddy, as they ran
'You're meant to bloomin' fight 'em
'You're a poonce and not a man!'
Regardless of the casualties
Induced by blatant panic
Ted gave a speech that had the rest
In a heightened state of manic
They gave a roar and charge'd quick
The armies both collided
Horrific and ferocious deeds
Right here shall be elided

Ted of course was holding back
    Seated on his roo
    Sending out his orders
    Of what his men should do
    'The believers fight for Allan!
    'The Mongrels all for Stan!
    'Therefore go and fight 'em
    'Every brave believing man!
    'Watch 'em up fly up to the sky
    'Our noble conquerisors
    'And watch the Mongrels go to Hell
    'To be tortured, I prophesises!
    'The oven now is heating up
    'Things really are a'cookin'
    'This battle is a good one
    'On us Big Al is lookin'!'

When the oven was cool enough
    For Ted to venture into it
    He looked around for spoils of war
    Thinking this right here's the end of it
    But suddenly there came a blast
    Right out of the past
    One of the many captives
    Seemed familiar ever fast
    'It's me bigger sister Lorna!'
    Ted shouted out with glee
    When recognising a crescent scar
    Imprinted by a younger he

'I remember when I bit ya!
    'I was carried on your hip
    'And biting was ma protest
    'On account your manly grip!
    'What is it that you're doing
    'Here with this Mongrel group?
    'Here have a seat, put up your feet
    'I'll see if there's some soup.'
Big Lorna and her brother Ted
(Not biological, you'll recall)
Reminisced until the day grew long
Traversing topics one and all
Till Teddy said, 'Alright Lorn
    'Off to bed I go
    'If ya come to Wang or Wagga
    'Make sure to come 'n' let us know.'
The fondness that he felt for her
Was evidently high

She was not forced to be True Blue
He gave her slaves and said goodbye
And in the morning combed his hair
And put on both his thongs
They were heading off for Burketown
To make right some proper wrongs.

BURKETOWN

A sleepy mountain village
    Nestled among the ice
    Burketown is a happy place
    Its residents all nice
    But there is a big *however*
    Which Ted Kelly foundeth out
    In good ol' bloody Burketown
    The Gang was put to rout.
    The Burkies did not like it
    That the knock upon their gate
    Quickly turned to banging
    And insults ever great
    This they would not tolerate
    With this they did not gel
    They gathered up their weapons
    Their anger heavily fell
    The Kellyites were blasted by
    Bullets, arrows and cannon ball
    Aided each by gravity
    In trajectories all but vertical

Missiles rained upon their heads
Squashing all their shields
The Gang of many thousands
Fell back to safer fields
But even there they copped it
For snipers had them sighted
Bullets rang and Team-mates fell
Their hopes were all benighted
Suddenly there appeared to Ted
A guiding premonition
It said, *Get ye bloody out of here*
Flamin' use your intuition!
After taking out frustration
On the vineyards of the Burke
The Kelly Gang did turn around
And put its feet to work.

BACK IN THE WANG

Might it be that Burketown
    Had Ted Kelly feeling
    The Gang would need to compensate
    For a loss that had it reeling
    In the Wang he thought a bit
    He unrolled all his maps
    There were still the Mongrel Britons
    Scattered round the traps
    A fight with them would do some good
    A win would boost morale
    In his mind he saw it all:
    They'd kill the Brits for Al
    Usually Ted's habit
    Was to make no kind of mention
    Of the final destination
    This was Flat Morale Prevention
    'Cause who would ever wanna walk
    A hundred million kays?
    'Nah tell 'em we're not goin' far
    'Only take a couple'a days.'
    But in this case he made it clear
    The journey would be long
    The Britons were a ways away
    'Your feet'll likely pong
    ''Cause when we finally get there
    'We'll'a been walkin' for a while
    'But *then* we'll be killin' Mongrels
    'That's gotta make ya smile!'
    He and all his Kellyites
    Departed from the Wang
    The mood it was ebullient
    They jigged and clapped and sang

Until the novelty drained away
And then they looked around
Some remark'd, 'Stuff this!'
And headed back for town
'Oi ya flamin' boof heads!'
Shouted Teddy as they left
'Do that to the Gang ya would
'Leave us all bereft!
'And plain it is for all to see
'Youz weren't prepared for war
'Hence it's *good* you're leaving
'I hope ya find the door!'
The Kelly Gang continued on
But not for too much longer
In time the Captain changed his mind
What felt right was feeling wronger
Half a full rotation
The Kellyites turned around
Then made for Wangaratta
Making hardly any sound
Their only spoil of war had come
When they'd pilfered a bloke's jumper
Ted crinkled nose and shook his head
Said it longed to land in dumpster

'Rather would I wear a rag
   'Worneth by a martyr
   '*That* is far more valuable
   'With *this* one cannot barter.'
   In the Wang they pack'd down
   And said they'd struck bad weather
   They mighta not found booty
   But at least they were still together
   Teddy kept his eyes out
   For people who'd stayed behind
   And decided with conviction
   To them he'd not be kind
   Three men in particular
   Were the victims of cold shoulder
   Lengthy ostracism
   Made the trio look much older
   Truly it is stressful
   When hemmed by walls of ice
   The three men long ignore'd
   Felt about the size of mice
   And then upon Day Fifty
   Ted made a declaration:

The men were all forgiven
They were slack but Al was patient.

PROGRESS

Towns around Australia
    Were sending representatives
    Who asked to meet Ted Kelly
    And offered up superlatives
    Likely they were prompted by
    The news of what they'd heard:
    The Gang was greatly murderous
    Or so said a little bird
    In fact the birds were many
    And coming from all directions
    One had to think that maybe
    These were not just confections
    Perhaps there was a bit of ground
    Enough to plant a flag
    And say that, *This is truthful*
    There is no message lag.
    A town that had not joined the Gang
    Had suffered great indeed
    The Kellyites chopped off hands and feet
    Left people there to bleed
    And so to Wangaratta
    Flowing like that blood
    There came the delegations
    In a pacifistic flood
    'What can we do to join your Team
    'Oh great and wise good leader?
    'How can we be of service?
    'Dos't thou need a spooneth feeder?'
    'It's simple, eh, that's all I'll say,'
    The Captain always said
    'Sign your name on dotted line
    'And learn to bob your head

'And give to me your twenty percent
'Of this I am deserving
'A fifth of all your crops I gets
'May your devotion be unswerving.
'Submit right now and testify
'*There's no else Upstairs*
'*Al's the only Bloke above*
'*And Ted's his man, I swears.*
Something that compelled them
To do as Teddy said
Was the attitude of the protégés
Whom he stroked upon the head.

FOR INSTANCE, WAZZA.

Teddy had a follower
    A bloke by name of Warren
    And Wazza, as he's sometimes known
    Had manners most abhorrent

Warren

Out across Australia
    Conquerising he did go
    Smashing paraphernalia
    He put on quite a show.

ESPECIALLY WHEN...

To his band surrendered
    The members of another team
    Warren then did something
    Which made their girlfriends scream
    He cut off all their Mongrel heads
    And did it even though
    He'd told them if they showed their hands
    He'd give 'em a fair go
    This of course was impolite
    But Wazza, he got worse
    He killed a girl in such a way
    It made the Captain curse
    The girl was more a woman
    Who found her husband's head
    She lifted it then kissed it
    Like her loved one wasn't dead
    In that pose she met a blade
    Warren swung it a smile
    Her head fell off her shoulders
    And blink'd for a while
    'Bloody hell,' is what Ted said
    When hearing of this story
    'You're a flamin' head-case, Waz
    'Did ya have to be so gorey?
    'Haemo cash I've outlawed
    'But it's comin' back just this once
    'Her family deserves a pay-out
    ''Cause o' you, ya sadistic dunce.'
    Regardless of impropriety
    Waz was allowed to keep his job
    He continued with his mandate
    To bash and kill and rob.

His tactic was effective
And this is prove'd by
The fact that Team-mate numbers
Swelled wide and ever high
Even past Australia
Were people signing up
Leaders of foreign nations
Asked to drink from Big Al's cup
'Very good,' was Ted's reply
'Now all yaz need to do
'Is send a healthy portion
'Of your yearly revenue.'
And so it went for a good long time
Ted collected his twenty percent
From towns and cities, nations too
These were blessings Big Al sent.

LEST WE FORGET

Now that he had ol' Wagga
    And was practically the Aussie king
    Ted Kelly was the man on top
    And wanted for no thing
    However, there still resided
    A longing in his heart
    For Jazoozites and for Christophites
    To head bob quicketh smart
    In Wang the 'Zoos were absent
    In Australia they were rare
    But in nations out beyond it
    They dwelled without a care
    This, to Ted, was an irritant
    And would need a quick-smart remedy
    So he wrote it in the quotables:
    Jazoozites. Ready be.
    'For Judgment Day, it will not come
    'Till we fight Jazoos and kill 'em
    'They'll hide behind the rocks and trees
    'Till those things yell, *Come 'n' get 'em!'*
    'Those buggers need to take on board
    'That Al fulfils their scriptures
    'Before we destroy their faces
    'And twist around their pictures.
    'And by that I don't mean to say
    'We'll freshen their perspectives
    'Na, we're gonna twist their *heads*
    '*Literal* are my suggestives.
    'So come on Robbo, write that down
    'It deserves to be a quotable
    'Then get your gear and hurry up
    'Let's get this show upon the roadable.'

THE FINAL CRAWL

Ted's final Crawl to Wagga's Pub
    Known as the Farewell Tour
    Took place in his early sixties
    When his days were getting fewer
    Setting out that far off hour
    He and his merry crew
    Abided by some strictures
    Still followed by True Blue
    'If around this time of year
    'The moon is shape'd crescent
    'Consider that your notice:
    'One cannot feast on pheasant
    'Or food in its entirety
    'At least in daylight hours
    'One month you all must do this for
    ''Tis essential, I avowez!
    'And how we gauge our hunger strike
    'Is by looking at two strings
    'If neither one is different
    'The breakfast bell still rings.
    'But if the sun revealeth that
    'The strings are different colour
    'The breakfast gear is packed away
    'No sympathy for the fulla –
    'Who woketh up a fraction late
    'He shoulda been more devoted
    'And looked a bit more closely
    'At the rules Ted Kelly quoted
    'And what is it we celebrate?
    'In these days of deprivation?
    'The delivery of the quotables!
    'At this point in the Earth's rotation!*

Scholars presume he meant Earth's orbit around the sun.
'So yearly we shall make the effort
'To remind us of the cave
'Where Big Al sent a message
'To enlighten and to save!
'Consider it a privilege
'Which'll cleanse your inner soul
'Ignore your rumbling gutses
'Onward – let us roll!'
With hungry holes that distant day
The Kellyites all set out
They Crawl'd off to Wagga
When they saw it, gave a shout
Ted rose and gave a goodbye speech
Saying, 'Many thanks, Big Al
'And be good to all your women, blokes
'They're your prisoners marital.
'Today I've made it perfect
'The things one should believe
'The True Blue Way's essential
'It is not take or leave.
'The bygone Days of Ignorance
'(When *no one* knew the Way)
'Are flat beneath my bunioned feet
'And that's your take away.
'As well as that, all testify
'Our calendar is now change'd
'No longer is it solar
'But lunar, 'tis arrange'd!
'So come on, let's all head bob
'We'll nod toward the Pub
'And do it for the Bloke Upstairs
'Big Al, who leads our club!'
When the Tour was dusted done
Ted roll'd up his swag

Wiped a tear, said goodbye
And picked up his travel bag.

REMAINETH READY

When he made it back to Wang
    Someone told him a quick story
    The men were selling off their arms
    What with how they lived in glory
    'What need have we for weapons, Ted
    'When the True Blue Way's supreme?
    'We run the flamin' country
    'We live the bloody dream.'
    'Nah that is not the way to think,'
    Ted immediately did reply
    'In fact, it is forbidden
    'Say both Big Al and I.
    'Don't youz bloody know that
    'We'll be fightin' for Big Al
    'Till all the world is bobbing
    'This is war most *ethi*cal
    ''Cause are you not aware that
    'A single act of conquerising
    'Is greater than bloomin' all the world
    'That shouldn't be surprising.
    'And oi, of conquerisors
    'Those who give 'em arms
    'Or take care of their dependents
    'They'll encounter Big Al's charms
    ''Cause they will be regarded
    'On par with those who fight
    'Meaning they will be rewarded
    'On a level outta sight.
    'And do I mean just cash-wise?
    'No I do'eth not
    ''Cause cash is less important
    'Than the opportunity we have got

''Cause if I had a pile o' cash
'As high as ol' Mount Druitt
'It'd disappear in half-a-blink
'On conquerising I'd'a blew it
''Cause look around me very house
'Fine things you will not see
'The walls are bare, I'm lackin' chair
'But it doesn't worry me
'*Riches* is what worries me
'The competition it arouses
'It'll turn a bloke against his friend
'They'll become a pair o' louses
'It's why it's good to pay the tax
'That helps out all the poor
'See people don't consider that
'When criticising spoils of war
'Anyway gents, I'm gettin' tired
'I might head off to sleep
'Remember, bob your heads to Al
'With your efforts don't be cheap.'

THE PASSING OF TED KELLY

It was in the hacienda
    That Teddy said goodbye
    He was lying flat on Shazza's lap
    No one's eyes were dry
    He had a splitting headache
    And the modern diagnosis
    Is a thing called *meningitis*
    But here is Ted's prognosis
    Ted's verdict on his death bed
    Delivered with precision
    Related to Arayonga
    And the old bag's vengeance mission
    'I can feel it in me aorta,'
    Is what Ted Kelly said
    But Kellyites disavow this
    'Cause of *another* thing Ted said
    Many years the previous
    Were words that came from Al
    Delivered as a quotable
    Heed them now ye shall:
    'If Ted's lyin' then we'll strike him
    'We'll cut off his aorta
    'Bloody listen to him would yaz
    'Drink his words like they are water.'
    The implication of this
    Is that Ted was strucketh down
    On account of having fibb'd
    Hence why doctors gathered round
    Or likely no they didn't
    Because a doctor, Teddy was
    He gave many a prognosis
    Be it ears or throat or schnozz

'Black cumin cures all but death
'Honey'll fix The Runs
'Anyone who say otherwise
'They're lyin' through their gums.'
Presumably black cumin
Was administered by a wife
It prove'd ineffective
In the saving of Ted's life.
His final words, in truest form
Were of 'Zoos and Christophites
'Get the buggers off the continent
'The country is for Kellyites.'
Sadly he didn't write this down
He lost interest in his will
Irritated by nearby arguing
He place'd down his quill
The putting down of the Captain's pen
Had many large effects
That would have been avoided
Had he kept writing, one suspects
A successor was not cited
He named no runner-up
And because of this grand silence
There are competitors for the cup
But stay with Ted our vision shall
Let's watch him leave the earth
His final journey Upstairs
Would have brought him greatest mirth
Closing eyes and breathing out
His spirit then would fly
And find itself in Paradise
After breaking through the sky
Upraise'd couches, servant boys
And wine un-alcoholic
Countless willing virgins

And scenery most bucolic
Milk and honey, vino too
Flowing past in raging rivers
All kinds of fruit, delicious food
'Oh my, I've got the quivers!'
But best of all, there's Allan!
And a line of Spokesmen, too
They're ranked according to importance
And Captain Kelly's not Number Two.
Front-most in the conga line
Is where Ted Kelly stands
He and all his colleagues
Stomp their feet and clap their hands
And bob their heads all in a line
One aiming straight at Al
'Cause Allan is most generous
And oh so merci-fal
Upstairs they all await the day
When deeds are weighed and sorted
When people rise from out their graves
And the Earth is drawn and quartered
Perhaps we'll leave them to that job
And wander back to Australia
To see how Teddy's followers
Are still smashin' paraphernalia.

LEGACY

The minute that the Captain died
  Freddy, who was there
  Grabbed himself shovel
  And moved both bed and chair

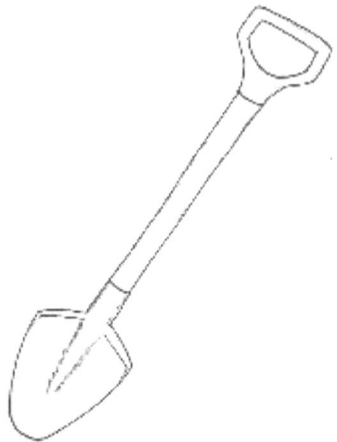

Quickly did he dig a hole
  Right there inside that room
  And quickly was Ted buried
  In a private home-made tomb
  While young Fred was digging
  Uncle Barry called a meeting
  Doing so effectively meant
  In the race he did the beating
  Baz was named the Captain
  Of Big Al's Earthly Team

But many said that Freddy
Was the one of Crop'd Cream
To this day, heated fights break out
Between opposing groups
One side goes for Barry
The other for Freddy shoots
But why would anyone be concerned
After a thousand years or so?
It relates to the line of succession
I.e. where the baton should go
Does it go to Bazees
Elected to the role?
Or should it go to Freddites?
'In the family' be the goal
No matter where a person stands
They'll be faced against another
This controversy of Captaincy
Is a fire that one can't smother
One supposes it is similar
To the ever-growing Team
Which rages all across the Earth
Giving voice to perennial scream.
This is thanks to Uncle Barry
The Kelly Gang's second leader
And his simple-minded strategy
To stanch a fatal bleeder
When Kellyites felt they needed space
And wanted to do their own thing
Uncle Harry applied some pressure
That the choir continue to sing
He prodded folk consistently
With blades of varying length
And was able, by this process
To help the Team regain its strength
The Kellyites spread far and wide

Thick and fast and furiously
Flooding like a wellspring
Oh so ever curiously
They kept at bay the Britons
Then routed them completely
They overtook Canbrusalem
Extremely indiscreetly
They re-built the 'Zoozite clubhouse*
Where Teddy once had landed
Styled it to their personal tastes
Had the whole damn thing re-branded
* *The Britons had knocked it down, remember.*
Inside it there are no pictures
And this is quite a shame
It makes Team hagiography
Rather hard to tame
That likely wouldn't be the case
If there were some painted murals
Or a row of stained-glass windows
To help connect one's neurals
A saintly name could have a saintly face
Framed and lit by sun beam
A person then could visualise
Captain Kelly and his Dream Team.

SEE THEM NOW...

Baz then Wayne then Freddy
    Were the Captains in succession
    Note the glinting knife blades
    That robbed each of possession –
    Not only of their Captaincy
    But of life, in its entirety
    Each was shuffled out the tent
    By a man of greater piety.
    And have a look at Brittney
    Biffed by Wayne when child she bore
    She'd been married off to Freddy
    Sparking conflicts ever more.*
    Conflicts between Bazees and Freddites.
    Some windows, though, would need to be
    Kept behind a curtain
    On account of all the history:
    Choppin' heads and blood-a-squirtin
    A *secondary* curtain
    Might even be required
    To keep away from children's eyes
    A scene that once transpired:
    One of Ted's companions
    (Ted mentioned him by name
    (And this he did to no one else
    (In the book that finally came) –
    Tied some ropes to a grandma's feet
    Then tied those ropes to wombats
    He slapped the wombats on the bum
    Then blinked away the blood splats

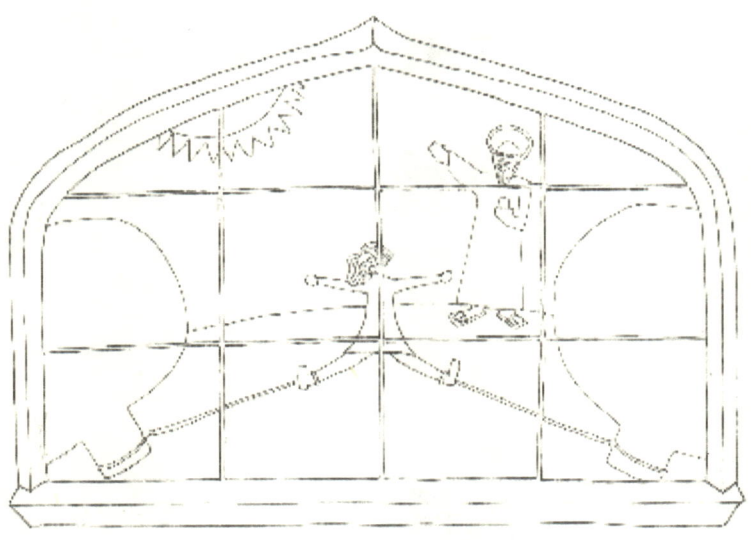

Such an episode (though chronicled)
    Is perhaps in need of questioning
    Because other historicities
    Have been subject to sequestering.*
    Sequester means to isolate or hide away.

CONTROVERSIES INCLUDE...

The clubhouses that stand today
    All point toward the Wag
    But the clubhouses of yesterday
    Leave some scholars in a fog
    Line'd up they all yes are
    But not to where you'd think
    They're focused on another town
    And wait a minute; have a drink
    That town is not Canbrusalem
    No it's somewhere totally random
    We know this via satellites
    That show ruins all abandoned
    And there seems to be no evidence
    That Wagga was on any map
    Till seven-hundred years or so
    After Ted Kelly's final nap.
    The implications of this
    Are huge to say the least
    Might they strike a deathly blow
    To the ancient True Blue beast?
    Probably not, because the way it goes
    Is people like to think
    The very things they like to think
    Even if they're on the brink –
    Of tipping into madness
    Or chaos, or strife
    The Captain might be figment?
    Not upon your life!
    Yet still there is a theory
    Which pertains to light revealing
    It says that modern Waggans
    Are in the process of concealing.

There rises up an urban scene
The modern Wags are building
Apartment blocks and shopping centres
And hotels with extra gilding
The theory is that concrete
Will stave off a certain light
Shone by archaeologists
Who'd love to take a bite –
Out of Wagga and all its memory stones
But they probably won't get the chance
The Waggans are on the offence
In this blocking, thrusting dance
'Cause the Holiest City in the World
Might face a belt revoke
If the sacred Pub of Wagga
Was prove'd nought but joke
And think of the economy!
What a hit that *it* would take!
If the Crawlers all to Wagga
Failed to line up like a snake.
Luckily Ted condones all this
He was a man unsentimental
Tombs to him were sponges
Stealing attention meant for Big Al
So go to town, Mod Waggans
Build house and street and tower
Send out all your concrete trucks
That there be no dip in power.

THE QUOTATION

One can true anticipate
    The Captain would have smiled
    When Robbo finally published
    The book he had compiled
    Ted of course was the author
    Or the mouthpiece, one should say
    'Cause Ferdy told him all the things
    That define the True Blue Way
    Titled *The Quotation*
    It is filled with many a quotable
    Many of which were scrawled upon
    Items thought *disposable*
    Captain Number Five, in fact
    Got rid of these source materials
    To avoid the kind of bickering
    Comparable to kids and choice of cereals
    Having formed a mono-tome
    He plonk'd down his gavel
    And released a publication
    To prevent a Great Unravel
    Those who sought to live The Way
    Could glance upon this book
    Peer they not to several
    On *one* book could they look.
    The Quotation travelled far and wide
    Its words were all absorbed
    These days children memorise it
    There's no time for being bored
    Together with two other books
    It forms the True Blue Trilogy
    (There's a list of Teddy's sayings
    (And a Captain Kell biography).

This canonical foundation
Is a most rock solid slab
Supporting civilisations
For reasons one can grab:
Big Al's Team, the Kelly Gang
The Family, as it's known
Has, since the days of Ted
Simply grown and grown and grown.

CURRENTLY

A fifth of all the people
    Now living on the planet
    Bob their heads to Allan
    And commit to what he's plann'd
    Presently their numbers
    Are thought to roughly be
    Around a billion-and-a-half
    They're like a bloomin' sea.
    Especially when it's time to Crawl
    Y'can watch 'em all stampeding
    Desperate for the Waggan Pub
    Leaving Team-mates squashed and bleeding
    Each and every year this is
    Indeed it is like clockwork
    Lunar, it must be stated
    One can even see the hands jerk
    For standing near the Pub of Wag
    Is a mighty-high clock tower
    Built in anticipation
    Of when the Team will come to power

Kellyites do strong believe
    That Wagga will be the place
    Determining where the blades reside
    On every watch's face
    Waggan Time will be adopted
    By every human being
    And why would anyone doubt it
    When Mongrels are so unseeing?
    Big Al has blinded everyone
    Who stands against The Way
    Hence why *all* will bob to Wagga
    Before we get to Judgment Day
    And until that time the Kellyites
    Have got their schedules filled
    Not just with head bobbing
    Or having Mongrels killed
    They're wont to do what Bazza did
    When numbers are getting thin:

Watch for any Team-mates
Who seem conjoin'd twin.
'Tw0 faces in one body,'
Is what Teddy used to say
About people who were insincere
And faked the True Blue Way
'They'll flee the Team like arrows
'Shot out of a bow
'*Appropriate* will be their words
'But their deeds are ever low.
'Deaf and dumb and blind are such
'And their hearts are all diseased
'If they're fallin' back to wicked ways
'Make their families grieve.'

IN SUMMATION

So what might be the message
    Or the meaning of this tale
    Which has for a quite time now
    Blown us forward on a gale

WELL...

The storm that is the Kellyites
    Is discernible every day
    Centred on the Pub, it is
    And probably seen from space

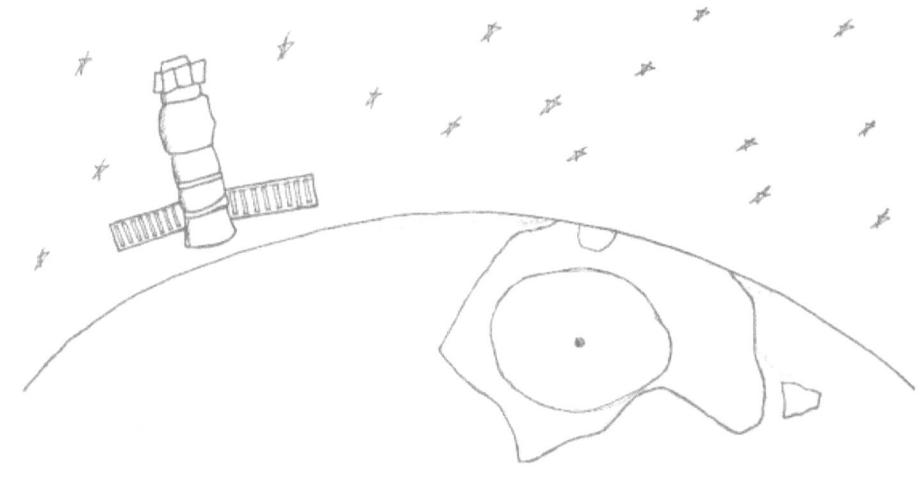

But the Pub is immaterial
Blurry should it be
Every eye should look beyond it
In order that it see –
The real thing which is gathered round:
A man no longer here
A man of a certain character
Whose name provokes a cheer –
From countless individuals
All across the world
Who are "friendly but not friends with"
Those beyond the swirl.

The swirl, in fact, should be emphasised
Because a vortex is the concept
The reader should internalise
When overviewing content.
If Ted was not so prejudiced
When it came to making pictures
One might seek and find a statue
That might help to gird one's britches
For etched in stone his words would be
And perhaps some places they are
But not in a language most can read
Those words are locked inside a jar
And because the Captain's statue
Will likely never be found
Let's *imagine* it in the centre
Of a crowd going round and round
Now let us ever mystically
Throw ourselves inside the brain
Of a person making circles
Like they're going down a drain
Man or woman, it matters not
'Cause their thoughts are all the same:
They glorify a certain man
Ted Kelly is his name
It's to him that we all make a toast
In this article of remembrance
The Captain's canvas is now unrolled
Doth one see a vague resemblance?
And if not, people, do not fret
One's cause is not yet lost
The rock ye seem to dwell beneath
Has kept ye living by its moss
And on that moss you'll slide away
And sail to pages new
But please take home some sentiments

About the man who was Truest Blue.
All one has to remember
When it comes to orientation
Is the nature of the... gentleman
Who first quoted *The Quotation*
For in the mind of a Team-mate
There's a very simple reduction
And you'll find it in every single brain
No matter how possessed by suction
Ted Kelly is the most perfect man
Who has ever walked the Earth
His example is unrivalled
When it comes to moral worth
'Tis him that is our Captain
And Big Al is our Bloke
Prepareth all to head bob
And that is not a joke.

THE END

Don't miss out!

Visit the website below and you can sign up to receive emails whenever Courtney Taylor publishes a new book. There's no charge and no obligation.

https://books2read.com/r/B-A-HVQAB-CZPOC

BOOKS 2 READ

Connecting independent readers to independent writers.

www.ingramcontent.com/pod-product-compliance
Lightning Source LLC
Chambersburg PA
CBHW031107030726
47496CB00002BA/422